I0760639

WOODSTOCK BOUND

STEVEN BATEMAN

4700 Millenia Blvd
Ste 175 #90776
Orlando, FL 32839

info@indieowlpress.com
IndieOwlPress.com

WOODSTOCK BOUND

Cover Design & Interior Layout by NightOwlFreelance.com

Paperback ISBN-13: 978-1-949193-77-0
Hardcover ISBN-13: 978-1-949193-78-7

For Woodstock!

Thank you for teaching us how Peace, Love, and Music can change the world for the better.

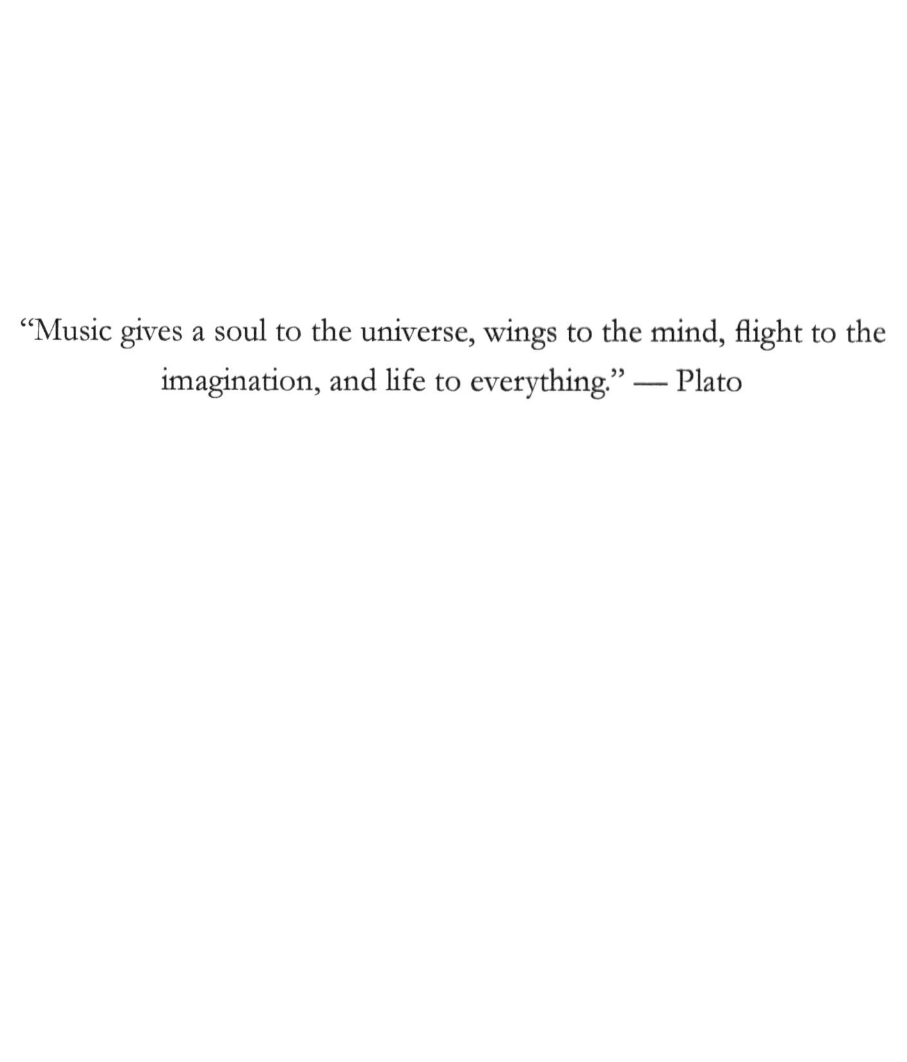

"Music gives a soul to the universe, wings to the mind, flight to the imagination, and life to everything." — Plato

PROLOGUE

Zac Taylor and his entourage moved like sheep following a shepherd. The massive crowd of concert-goers hiked up a steep hill they believed would lead them to Woodstock '94. Nearing the top, people began pointing upward. Following the fingers, they observed a tall sign—not yet readable from their current distance. "What do you think it says?" Jax asked. Other patrons were asking each other the same question, curious—not only with what the sign read but what might be waiting for them beyond it. They continued to climb upward, feeling fatigued and gasping for air. Eventually, the words were in focus. It was a large, white sign with dark-blue lettering, standing about twelve feet high and ten feet wide, reading from top to bottom:

WELCOME TO WOODSTOCK '94
SAUGERTIES, NY

Chills rushed through Zac's body. He looked down at his arms; every hair was standing erect, a feeling he commonly referred to as "Spidey-sense." Glancing down and to his right at Melany's arm, her hand firmly gripping Zac's, he noticed the hair on her arm was doing the same. Everyone who had made the journey—even the people Zac and his friends had picked-up along the way—had similar facial expressions.

They were smiling, yet these weren't regular everyday smiles, or smiles of amazement and curiosity; they were smiles of arrival. They all stood directly underneath the welcoming sign, in one line, side-by-side, then Jax blurted, "Holy hell!" It was the perfect statement for a group that was observing the most beautiful sight they had ever encountered. Zac couldn't have said it better himself as he looked upon the North Stage of Woodstock '94, scanning the massive crowd in every direction. He could not stop thinking how his journey to this point had begun five days ago with a rude awakening on his 18th birthday.

WOODSTOCK BOUND

CHAPTER 1

THE RUDE AWAKENING

Zac's bedroom door flew open with almost enough force to knock it off its hinges, slamming into the green wall behind it. Jumping up as if a tornado had entered his room, he looked around, foggy-eyed and confused. In the doorway stood Zac's stepdad, Rick, wearing nothing but his tighty-whities, a white t-shirt, and what appeared to be a florescent shotgun.

"Five a.m. Must be a peach of a dream," Rick stated with a contrived southern drawl.

Rick thought it was humorous to quote and act out scenes from popular movies, hands-down his favorite pastime. This morning he was in rare form as Doc Holiday. "Why, Zac, you look like you're ready to burst."

"Get out!" Zac demanded as he tried to orient himself.

"Well, I suppose I'm deranged, but I assume I'll have to squirt you with my Super Soaker. Cover your ears, darlin'."

The harsh whine of water pressurizing in the plastic barrel of Rick's

Super Soaker failed to prepare Zac for what was about to happen. Squirt!

"Isn't that a daisy?" Rick laughed to himself, now holding the Super Soaker at his side, as if he were Sylvester Stallone in *Rambo*.

Zac did not share in the amusement, and Rick's impersonation of Val Kilmer's character from *Tombstone* failed miserably to impress as ice-cold water seeped through his queen-sized *Thundercats* bedspread. "You're an ass, not Doc Holiday!" Zac shouted with a deep hatred in his voice.

"Why, Zac, are we cross? Does this mean we're not friends anymore? You know, Zac, if I thought you weren't my friend, I don't think I could bear it." He walked next to the nightstand on the left of Zac's bed and sat the Super Soaker down, tapping it gently twice. "There, now we can be friends again. I calculate that's the end of this rude awaking," he said with a snicker.

"Why don't you jump on your horse and get the hell out of my room!" Zac demanded, throwing the wet blankets to the floor.

Rick paused, looked over his right shoulder as he was about to exit the room and said, "Don't plan much for the rest of your summer."

"Why's that?"

"Cause the concluding weeks of summer are reserved for the last charge of Zac Taylor and his immortals. Well, then, good day." Rick exited the room laughing to himself.

What a dick, Zac thought as he pushed the power button on his radio/CD player on the top of his dresser, sitting under the only window in his bedroom. "And what the hell did he mean by *the last charge of Zac Taylor and his immortals*?" Opening the curtains, he was greeted with a warm Oklahoma dawn, the sun beginning to rise in the east. The end of the song, "No Rain," by Blind Melon blared from the speaker. Reaching down to pick up his soaked comforter, all he could do was chuckle at the irony. Anger felt pointless as he placed it in his hamper, which "screamed" to be emptied. The song concluded, and the DJ's voice came over the radio announcing something about Woodstock '94. Zac didn't obsess over the announcement, but he did think to himself, *how cool would it be to attend that!?* Like all soon-to-be high school seniors, this was his last summer before graduating, and he wanted to experience something legendary. Woodstock '94 certainly fit into the legendary category. However, Rick, clearly had other plans for the remainder of his summer vacation.

Zac jumped in the shower, soaking his shoulder-length blond hair as the warm water flowing from the showerhead cascaded over his six-foot-two frame. Looking down at his feet, he could not believe how tan his skin was after two months of lifeguarding at the city pool—all except for his bright white ass.

Ring, ring! "Shit," he mumbled as the phone rang. One ring down: he only had four more before the answering machine picked up the call. He leapt out of the tub, almost tangling himself in the shower curtain, missing the floor mat entirely, and grabbed a towel. Sprinting down the hallway, he tried to stop as he grabbed the doorknob with his left hand. He failed to calculate his momentum properly—plus, wet feet and hands. Zac's feet flew out from underneath him. He hit the floor. Hard. Landing flat-backed knocked the air out of his lungs. *What the fuck,* he thought, lying naked on the cold hardwood floor, his left hand still clenched to the doorknob. He heard the third ring. One ring remaining. In severe pain, he popped up, leaving the towel on the floor, hoping to retrieve the call before the final ring. It may seem peculiar to endure so much to answer a phone call, but rule number one in his life was never to miss a call or a page. He could not count on his family to answer because, like most teenagers living at home, the phone was usually for him, and they didn't care to speak with his friends.

Zac retrieved the phone receiver before the fourth ring, but his intended triumphant, "Hello" fell short due to the oxygen depletion in his lungs. "Zachary?" the voice on the other end questioned. Besides his mother, there was only one person who referred to him as Zachary.

"Uncle J!" His uncle J, or Uncle Jimmy, was someone he respected deeply, considering him more of a father figure than that of an uncle. Coming into manhood, Zac was often confused about things, and not having any siblings—and a dickhead of a stepdad—did not provide many avenues for him to discuss his perplexities. However, Uncle Jimmy was always there for him, even if not in person. If Jimmy were across the country and Zac reached out by paging him, he would stop everything to call and listen and give the best advice possible.

"Are you done working that summer job yet, son?" Uncle J's question was somewhat muffled by static coming from his end of the line, as if he were on a payphone.

"Not yet—we have two-and-a-half weeks left."

"Ah, the last weeks of working the city pool. Appreciate every second, son; it will be over before you know it," Jimmy added.

"Where are you? Are you stopping by to see us at all before the summer ends?" Zac asked, hoping to hear a yes.

"I need to speak with your mom, Zachary."

Looking over at his alarm clock, Zac noticed he was running late, so he didn't press the issue. He yelled for his mother, said his goodbyes, then got back to his shower.

While getting dressed, Zac thought about his Uncle J and how on his mother's side of the family he was considered an outcast, "a byproduct of the sixties," they would say. His parents had never quite come to terms with the fact that their only son had matriculated to Berkley. After Uncle J completed his undergrad degree, he obtained a law degree from Berkley as well, yet never practiced a single day in his life. He began selling memorabilia at *Grateful Dead* shows and in beach towns up and down the California coast. Not exactly the path Uncle J's father planned for him when shelling out the high cost of college tuition. Nevertheless, he managed to make a very nice living.

CHAPTER 2

COLLEGE FOR BREAKFAST

Zac's mother, Janis, was in the kitchen spreading sugar on a grapefruit and enjoying a hot cup of coffee when he joined her. She was only 48-years-old; however, to him she seemed ancient. She too could be described as somewhat of a "free spirit." She often informed those that complemented her on her name that she was named after the rock legend, Janis Joplin: her favorite singer. However, anyone that took the time to do the math in their heads could quickly conclude the numbers didn't add up, and that wasn't the case. Her folks contend that they wanted both of their children's names to start with the letter J. Nonetheless, similar to her older brother, Jimmy, her parents referred to her as "a byproduct of the sixties" as well.

She considered herself somewhat of a "flower-child," partially because she was a bit of a hippie, but mostly because she was the assistant manager at the only flower shop in Weatherford, Oklahoma; a job that brought her tremendous joy. She frequently wore pastel sundresses, a fashion that complemented her long golden-blonde hair and slender, toned body. Zac hated to admit it, but his mother was beautiful. And he could never wrap his head around how a woman like her ended up with a guy like Rick. In his eyes, she was way too good for the rent-a-cop.

Rick, on the other hand, was a 47-year-old, balding, dark-haired man who stood six-feet tall with a beer-belly he'd acquired after years of drinking any acholic beverage he could get his hands on. Rick was an acholic, and a mean-ass drunk to boot. Rick wasn't physically abusive, but his temper usually got the best of him, and his verbal assaults were renowned. An abuse that he often took out on Zac. He was unhappy with his job as a security guard for the local strip mall. A dead-end job for a man that was mean as shit to everyone, excluding Janis.

He worked long, hard hours but seemed to always make time for Janis. When Janis spoke about how they had met, she would say times were different back then. Zac was only two-years-old at the time, so he had no way of really knowing, but she argued that Rick had won her over by his propensity to "stand up for the little guy." Apparently, he hated seeing people being taken advantage of. This had somehow become the main reason she fell for him. He once had the ambition of becoming an attorney—to help "the little guys" from being mistreated, but Janis said life had got in the way and he took the only, somewhat decent paying, job he could with a high school diploma. She always said, "The world changed, and we had to change with it."

Zac never understood where she was going with "the world was changing" bit, but that was her story. Even though he was the only father figure Zac had ever known since being abandoned by his biological father when he found out Janis was expecting, Rick had never done anything to win Zac over the way he had Janis, so Zac only felt disgust for Rick.

Wearing a sly smile, Janis questioned, "Did Rick wake you this morning?"

Giving her a piercing stare, Zac replied, "When is that guy going to get off my back?"

"Zachary, he doesn't mean anything by it. He's trying to be funny."

Believing that Rick was anything but funny, Zac pulled a chair out from under their small oak kitchen table and took a seat to the left of his mother. Quietly, he ate his traditional breakfast: Honeycomb cereal.

Trying to break the awkward silence, Janis asked, "So what do you think about taking a few college courses this year, baby?"

Zac glared at her with his right eyebrow raised. "Yeah right, like that's ever gonna happen."

She had been mentioning college classes for weeks, trying to prepare him for his future and possibly early graduation. She had hoped he would graduate college early, for she was a firm believer that one should experience some sort of adventure before delving into corporate America. Janis believed Zac graduating early would offer such an opportunity.

Zac did exceptionally well with his studies and had the potential to get a scholarship in soccer, or possibly as a pianist. His mom had insisted he learn an instrument, putting him in lessons at the young age of six. He knew his family couldn't afford to help him do anything remotely adventurous, though. They scraped by, living paycheck to paycheck, like most families did in his small town. If he were to attend college, it would be on his own merit.

"You know, you might actually enjoy entering college early. Besides, Melany's mother told me the other day that she will be taking a few college courses this upcoming semester."

Janis always had a way of mentioning Melany Summers when she was trying to bait Zac into doing things against his will. Melany and Zac had been friends since they were in diapers. Over the years, she had transformed into the kind of girl who gave teenage boys wet dreams. Being smart, funny, and athletic were only a few of Melany's strongest attributes—not to mention she was the best drummer in their high school band. She wore her curly reddish-brown hair long. Often down, flat-ironed into waves, it gracefully framed her flawless, porcelain-doll skin. Even disheveled, she was adorable. If not tamed, her wild curly locks would best a black man's afro any day of the week; she could even hold a pick in it while jogging. Zac had frequently pushed her to pursue a career in commercials because of her perfect smile. His favorite scenario for her was as a fast food spokesperson. He said watching her eat was hypnotic since she always seemed to take the ideal bite, making the food look delicious. He would, however, give her shit about the size of her teeth; they weren't huge, but her smile was big, which bore a striking resemblance to the Cheshire Cat in *Alice in Wonderland.* For her sixteenth birthday (two days after Melany had her braces removed), Zac gave her a bright-red one-foot toothbrush with clear one-inch bristles, claiming it would do a better job than an average person's toothbrush.

Melany and Zac's mothers had been childhood friends as well, which was the primary reason he lived in Oklahoma. The two women had made a deal as children to do whatever it took to reside in the same town as adults. A promise Janis made a reality when Rick landed his security guard gig the year Zac entered the second grade. To Zac, Melany was, by far, the most exciting and beautiful girl he had ever met. Unfortunately, he resided in the "friend zone," with no chance of relocating in sight.

Looking over at his mother, Zac thought to himself, *Great! My junior year has been over for little over two months, but Rick and Mom already have the remainder of my summer—and my senior year—mapped out.* He needed to change the subject and went with the first thing that came to mind. "What did Uncle J have to say?"

"You mean Jimmy?" Rick said, emerging from the hallway as he buttoned the top button of his gray and brown uniform shirt. "Is that who was on the phone?"

Janis answered, "Yes, dear. He doesn't think he's going to be able to visit this summer: business."

Rick could not refrain, "He's a daisy if he does." He winked at Zac.

"He's not coming?" Zac shook his head in disbelief.

"Not this time, honey. He has two Grateful Dead shows to get to, one in Vermont and the other in DC. I know you really wanted to see him, but he does very well at those performances."

Zac's right shoulder throbbed a bit from the fall earlier, and he hoped the rest of his day didn't follow suit with everything that had transpired thus far. *Today is off to a really shitty start,* he thought.

CHAPTER 3

THE BOAT RIDE

Zac's family lived in what some would describe as an apartment community; however, that was being generous. Each complex was one level, offering tenants either a two or three-bedroom space. Zac's family lived in one of the three-bedroom units—not exactly the home he desired to live in. He was a bit jealous that two of his closest friends lived in what he considered to be mansions. Regardless of how hard he had to work to make his dream home a reality, he always told himself that he'd never live in an extravagant place as an adult. Still, he'd like to have the choice. For the most part, his was a "quiet" neighborhood, which he appreciated. That is until Jax, his best friend, pulled up in front of Zac's apartment to retrieve him on days they were scheduled to work at the city pool.

As usual, Jax pulled up in front of Zac's parents' apartment honking the horn in his midnight-blue, white-topped, 1960 Lincoln Continental—the last of the big Lincolns. Jax pushed the limit when it came to honking his horn. Blaring it with a quick release couldn't satisfy the devil deep within his soul—that kind of shit was for pussies, in his mind. He usually held the horn down until either Zac came outside, or his arms tired from keeping the pressure on it. Either way, the horn was blasting almost every morning in front of Zac's apartment for a solid two to three minutes. Rick loathed the way Jax whaled on the horn, but that made it funny to Zac and always put a smile on his face.

"Damn that little shit!" Rick hollered as the startle from the honk almost made him spill coffee on the only clean work shirt he had left for the day. "You better tell that knucklehead to stop honking that damned horn when he pulls up!" Rick pointed at Zac to throw emphasis on the demand. Zac pushed his chair out from under the table, grabbed his backpack, kissed his mom on her forehead, smirked at Rick, then bolted to meet Jax outside.

Jax's ride was commonly referred to as "the boat" because of its enormous size. The boat could easily sit six people, but Jax and his friends had often piled ten-plus inside on their journeys, especially when he snuck friends into places like the local drive-in. As Zac approached the boat, Jax jumped up, peering from the sunroof and yelled with his arms wide open, "Happy birthday my brother from a fine-ass mother!"

Zac opened the passenger door with a smile, threw his backpack on the floorboard, and took his place as the co-captain of the vessel. "Thanks, brother, I really appreciate it."

"Z, is Rick home?" Jax asked.

"Yeah, what's up?"

"What did he say this time?" Referring to the multiple times he had honked his horn.

"Lay off the damn horn, my neighbors are trying to sleep."

"Fuck that!" Honk! Jax laughed and then laid into Zac, "Why are you always late, Z? I'm here every damn day at 6:30, and you're always late. Its fucking Sunday, brother, you know I shave that fine ass mother of yours back on Sunday's."

Jax was the son of the Weatherford Postmaster. A title that sounded cool, but, in a small town, wasn't remotely distinguished. His father was a lot like Rick, an asshole. Which was one of the main reasons Zac and Jax became so close over the years. They truly needed each other, not only for friendship, but for emotional support from all the hell their dad's had put them through as children. However, Jax's father was an asshole that actually beat the shit out of Jax when his temper flared up. In their chats over the years, Zac came to believe Jax's father blamed him for his mother leaving him when Jax was four. Being that Weatherford was such a small community, like most Oklahoma towns, everyone had their suspicions of the abuse Jax received, especially when he was younger. Yet, Jax still loved his father, he was all the guy had, and wouldn't even think about "narcing" on him. Zac and his other friends also believed when his mother left his family, Jax had a tough time trusting females. The number-one reason they believe contributed to Jax becoming a womanizer.

Nevertheless, Jax was the best friend a guy could ask for and would give you his right arm if you needed it. He was average height, about six foot and stocky as hell for someone that had not played sports since Little League Baseball—or done anything remotely resembling physical activity for that matter. Jax did, however, have one characteristic that most found somewhat peculiar. He was obsessed with The Beatles. Everything Jax did, mimicked the rock icons. He even decorated his room as a crosswalk, so it would look like the cover of their *Abbey Road* album. His hair was bushy, identical to the way the band wore theirs back in the sixties. Many thought he was trying to emulate the up-and-coming group *Oasis'* look, but in his eyes, those were fighting words. During their junior year, the high school hosted a career day. The idea was to help students figure out what they wanted to do after graduation.

Most people talked about becoming doctors or lawyers, not Jax. He told anyone that would listen, "I'm going to start a Beatles tribute band and tour the world singing classic Beatles songs." He did have mad skills on the guitar and produced terrific vocals, so it was not too farfetched that he might actually pursue that as a profession. To prove how good he was, he persuaded his entire crew, most of whom played some sort of musical instrument, to enter the Weatherford High School talent show their junior year. Pretty easy to guess what band they covered. Still, they all got up in front of the entire school, hell, the whole community, and crushed the competition, easily taking first place. Second place went to a singing baton twirler, who dropped the baton twice before her act ended. It would be safe to say that moment was one of Jax's most significant accomplishments in high school, as he didn't do as well as the others academically.

Jax did, however, have a habit of taking his obsession to the extreme at times, much like his horn honking. If you ever brought up listening to something other than The Beatles while the boat was in motion, you'd be sure he would leave your ass on the curb, that's no shit! About two months ago, Jax took Jessica Hartman out to the movies, or in literal terms, he attempted to go to the movies with her. She thought it would be a great idea to pull a CD out of her handbag for them to listen to along the way. Jax quickly shouted, "Woman, what the fuck are you doing!?" Jessica replied, "I don't like The Beatles…" and before she could even finish her sentence, the boat came to a screeching halt on Main Street. Jax reached across Jessica's lap, unbuckled her seatbelt, and opened the passenger door, forcing her out. He sped off laughing to himself while listening to "Let It Be," leaving her ass on the curb, gangster style—or at least that's how he tells the story.

The two were driving down the road when Zac started opening every compartment he could see, searching for a Marlboro Light, "You got a dagwood for me?" Zac asked.

"Damn, broke ass, when you gonna buy your own damn grits? I'm tired of supporting your ass! You're 18 now, buy your own damn smokes."

Getting pissed, Zac glared at Jax who then pointed to the glovebox, the only spot Zac had not looked.

"So what did the fam get you for your birthday?" Jax questioned.

"Not a damn thing, man, I didn't even get so much as a happy birthday from my mom or Rick," Zac responded.

"That's a disgrace, my friend. Well, shit, man, today is going to be a day you won't ever forget, and tonight, well, let's say tonight is going to be epic. I guarantee it!" Jax smiled and reached out to squeeze Zac's left shoulder.

On the way to scoop up Double Dee, or Double for short, known to others as Michael Stephenson, Zac rolled a joint from the quarter ounce he pulled out of his backpack so they could smoke on their way to the pool. Double at the time was the only black kid in Weatherford. He was the same height as Jax but was the only one of the crew who could grow a beard. Something he rarely shaved because he had Pseudo Folliculitis Barbae. A fancy name for someone that has persistent irritation, bumps, on their face caused by shaving. He's referred to as Double Dee for one reason only, he possessed the largest man-tits they had ever seen on a kid.

They first met Double sitting on the bench in Little League. During games, Double would ask kids he didn't like random questions, such as how many push-ups his dad could do. He once asked this question to Lonnie Johnston—the kid on the team who was only there because his parents wanted him to make friends, knowing damn well Lonnie possessed zero athletic skills whatsoever. Lonnie guessed that Double's dad could do 50 push-ups. Double quickly made a face that resembled Bruce Banner right before transforming into the Hulk and shouted, "My dad has no arms, mother-fucker!" Subsequently, he ran over and began showcasing how easily his large frame could squeeze the air out of a much smaller person. Both Zac and Jax knew Double's father had two perfectly good working arms, but they thought that shit was funny as hell and instantly befriended him. It also did not hurt that Double was usually the only one who had money for the snack bar and he always let Zac and Jax mooch off him.

Double's father was one of three Douglas County judges, and many thought, because of Double's intellect, he would inevitably follow in his father's footsteps and someday practice law. However, Double's passions focused on architecture and music. He quickly became frustrated when his size prevented him from being comfortable in small places. In his eyes, becoming an architect would help him combat this frustration. His backup plan was to become a famous saxophonist. He was the only sax player in the high school band, and, like Zac, began taking lessons at a very early age. Zac had to admit that when it came to music, he was the first to stereotype Double's favorite music genera. He thought for sure Double would be into gangster-rap, because he was black. However, nothing could be further from the truth. While he loved rap, like all of his friends did, especially Cypress Hill, NWA, and E-40, Double was a huge Kenny G fan.

The neighborhood where Double's family lived was often referred to as the Robin Leach Development, or RLD for short because every house looked like it could be on an episode of *Lifestyles of the Rich and Famous*. It was a gated community right off of Interstate 40; most of the homes were enormous, easily three stories, not including a basement. The basements, if finished, meant the houses were four stories, of which 90% of them were. Each one was equipped with a wraparound driveway, three car garages, and a heated pool, which some locals said made the homes "more elegant." When driving through the development, Zac and Jax often felt like they were trespassing because they weren't driving a Mercedes or BMW.

They pulled up to Double's house and utilized the wraparound driveway that led almost to the front door of his home and noticed Double was shutting the mostly stained-glass double-doors behind him. "Awe fuck!" Jax yelled, as if he were being pulled over by the authorities. Zac looked at him, paranoid because he had his sack of weed out on his lap, having just finished rolling the joint he had started when leaving his neighborhood. Still confused, Zac asked, "What the fuck, man?" Zac followed Jax's pointing finger to Double's location. "What the hell is he wearing?" Zac immediately questioned.

Double was dressed in unusual fashion this morning. Sporting a bright-red polo shirt; however, he had his collar flipped up. Both Zac and Jax instantly knew he had flipped it up on purpose. It wasn't something that could go unnoticed on Double, like forgetting to fold his collar down, this was an intentional fashion statement. Double looked as if he had reinvented the turtleneck.

"There is no way that tubby bastard is getting into my ride wearing that shirt like that!" Jax protested.

Rolling down his window as Double approached the boat, Zac stated in a cool tone, "What up Kool-Aid?" Zac had nailed it, Double looked exactly like the Kool-Aid man, shorts and all.

Jax began laughing uncontrollably, "He does look like the Kool-Aid guy!" Adding, "He's got that lame ass smile and everything."

Not to be capped on without a fight, Double quickly interjected as he opened the rear passenger side door and took his seat, sinking the boat about 3 inches with his 350-pound frame, "Fuck you, punk asses. I popped my collar, fools, I can't help it if you hick-ass mother-fuckers got no fashion sense."

On their way to pick up Melany—their last stop before heading to work, Zac sparked up the joint he'd rolled. The joint was rolled flawlessly, the weed finely cut-up and well distributed throughout the Zig-Zag rolling paper, making it burn smoothly as it was passed between the three.

"Who the fuck says shit like that, popped my collar?" Jax blurted out in his best Double impersonation, as the song "We Can Work It Out" echoed through the boat speakers: a song perfect for the occasion.

Double and Zac, plagued with a severe case of the giggles, lost it. It wasn't because of what Jax had asked, it was because of the timing. The moment he asked, the first lyrics of "We Can Work It Out" began. Jax didn't catch the irony, but Zac and Double did.

Zac turned over his left shoulder so he could see Double, passed him the joint and greeted him with a smile, and raised right eyebrow, and a nod. They never had to say a word.

Double grabbed the joint from Zac's hand and started hitting it like he had bought the damn thing.

"I swear to God, Kool-Aid, I'm about to lose my shit on your tubby ass!" Jax exclaimed, smacking his dashboard, "You hit then pass, hit then pass. It's not rocket science, and if it were, I'm sure that big ass brain of yours could comprehend such a simple process!"

Double observed Jax, waiting for his smart ass to say something else.

As he watched him Double resorted to his Bruce Banner intimidation expression.

"Jax, keep that shit up, I dare you! I'm twice you and Z's size, I have to hit a few more times than you, I weigh more. How else am I gonna get mines!"

Zac and Jax looked at one another confused, as if they couldn't believe that was the best argument Double could produce.

Zac couldn't resist. "Mr. Kool-Aid, may I call you Kool-Aid? You do know that this isn't alcohol, right? I don't think the same weight rules apply regarding the amount one has to ingest to get the same effect as another. Now, had you posed the argument that the size difference in one's lung capacity could result in a larger person needing to inhale more than that of a smaller one, I think myself and my co-counsel, Jax, here, would have bought what you were selling. Hell, you could have randomly used the word diaphragm—I would have given you that. However, you'll have to forgive me, counselor, but I'm going to have to overrule your objection."

Jax gave Zac a high-five, adding, "My caucasian!"

Double leaned forward in his seat, "What the fuck did you call him?" Double asked. Jax had a frog in his throat, "Um—my caucasian?"

Double pressed, "So what am I, Jax—huh?

Jax looked over to Zac for another assist, "Oh, don't look at Z, big boy. What am I—huh, Jax?"

Jax said nothing, "Un-huh! That's what I thought—pussy!"

Zac held his left hand up in the back seat, and Double skinned it. "I hope you enjoy my spit, too, mother-fuckers! And ya'll best stop calling me Kool-Aid!" Double said as he passed the saliva-soaked roach to the front seat.

They arrived at Melany's house and knew they would be waiting a while, so they parked near the curb in front of her home, which was directly under a tall oak tree that easily cast a shadow across three-fourths of the street. Sitting under the shade of the oak tree in her front yard, they finished smoking the joint that Double had saturated. Melany lived only a few neighborhoods over from Zac, and it would seem logical to pick her up first since Double lived across town. However, their morning rituals consisted of smoking a joint before work, and Melany never partook in what seemed to be their favorite pastime. That, and her being the head lifeguard, and high on duty was pretty frowned upon. As they sat there, stoned out of their minds, Luke Baker, and two of his friends pulled up in Luke's light blue 1976 Ford LTD, which was a boat as well, yet not nearly as classy as Jax's ride.

Luke really wasn't someone they considered a friend, more of an acquaintance. Nevertheless, he usually had dope parties because his parents traveled a great deal for his father's business. This usually meant Luke and his older brother, Steve, who happened to be 21, were fending for themselves a majority of the time. Jax peered over and used his left index finger to roll his window down to chat with Luke and company. "What up, Z?" Luke shouted across to his friend sitting shotgun.

Zac exhaled a cloud of smoke and returned the what's up. "What am I, chopped liver?" Jax shouted because Luke had bypassed him and greeted Zac.

"Fuck you, Jax!" Luke replied before informing the three of them that he would be hosting a birthday bash in honor of Zac's 18th, starting around 8 o'clock that evening. Enlightening them on the fact Steve had already picked up the keg, which was sitting on ice as they spoke. "That's marvelous, brother, thank you!" Zac exclaimed.

Jax looked over at Zac then back at Double and back at Zac, "Are you guy's not gonna fucking ask? I have to know," Jax announced. Jax turned toward Luke's LTD, crossing his arms on the window sill and resting his chin on his arms, as if he were a boy in love, his head cocked to the left, "Luke, is your mom gonna to be there?"

Luke scowled and peeled out.

"Why you always got to do that shit, man?" Zac questioned.

Double was in the backseat laughing his ass off, tears ran down his face. Both Zac and Jax simultaneously turned in his direction, "What?" They both asked in unison. "I thought you were going to ask what kind of beer was in the keg," Double replied. They all shared a laugh, then Jax said, "It better be Bud!" All three shouted together with their heads up and arms open, "Cause if we ain't smoking Bud, we're drinking Bud!"

Still waiting on Melany, they sat in silence for what seemed an eternity. Out of nowhere, Double posed the question, "What are you guys looking for in the perfect girl?" Zac and Jax looked at each other with a *what-the-fuck kind of question was that* look on their faces. Double continued, "I want a girl that likes me for me, if she happens to have bigger tits than me, that would be a perk—perky titties!"

Trying to avoid Jax from capping on Double, Zac quickly added, "Man, I want a girl that will call me up out of the blue and ask me to come over, watch movies, and get naked. We wouldn't even have to do anything sexual, just the two of us being completely comfortable with who we are, almost as if we were one." Double looked up at the ceiling, resting his head on the backseat headrest and let out a deep breath. "That some deep shit, Z."

From the corner of his left eye, Zac could see Jax was looking at him, then turned to Double, then back to Zac, then back again to

Double. "What is wrong with you dipshits? We need to be like Don on *Dazed and Confused* and fuck as many chicks as we can while we are stuck in this place!" Jax protested.

As Zac turned toward Jax to retort, a soft sexy voice, one he had described many times to Jax as the voice of angel entered his right ear from behind. "Is that all you think about, Jax?" Melany asked. Her voice sent shivers through Zac's body. It didn't matter what she said, her voice always had that effect on him. "Happy Birthday, Zac," she quickly added, touching his right arm.

The morning breeze sent the scent of her sunblock rushing through Zac's nose. She didn't wear the standard sunblock one would pick up at the local drugstore, her aunt in Florida sent it to her. It smelt like coconut and vanilla. Jax always said it smelt like sweaty balls; no matter, if that were the case, Zac loved the smell of sweaty balls. Melany was wearing her usual lifeguard attire: a red one-piece bathing suit and black lifeguard shorts, tan Dr. Martin sandals, black Ray-Ban sunglasses, and a white visor with her curly hair pulled back in a ponytail.

Jax, being the smartass he is, could not resist, "Why, Mel, you gonna help me with that?"

She did not respond; her simple middle finger communicated loud and clear.

"Fuck me, Happy Birthday, Z! I meant to say something when Luke brought it up, but I'm so fucked up I forgot. Ain't short-term memory loss a bitch!"

Melany jumped, as she hadn't noticed Double sitting in the backseat. "Jesus, Mike, I didn't even see you back there."

Jax, again, could not refrain, "Why the hell do you call him Mike, his name is Double Dee. For fuck-sake, Mel, it's like I'm your old man telling you to turn off the goddamn lights all the time; you never get it." The boat shook violently as Double flipped up his Kool-Aid shirt, and, with no shame, flashed all three of them. Proving, once again, why he had been bestowed the nickname.

Melany walked around to the driver's side door, opened it, and signaled for Jax to exit the boat. "That's what I'm talking about!" Jax said, spreading his legs, grinning from ear-to-ear. "Get in the back stoned-ass, I'm not letting you drive me. You know the drill. And for the record, there is no way in hell I'm calling a guy with bigger tits than me Double Dee." Jax knew she would not budge, so he did what any wise man would do in that situation, he took his stoned ass to the backseat and sat next to Double.

"Call me Kool-Aid now, bitch, I dare your ass," Double whispered to Jax as he moved his backpack out of Jax's way. Zac looked over at Melany, and in the calmest voice he could muster asked, "You think you can handle this big thing, Mel?" She looked to her right toward Zac with her twinkling bluish-green eyes and said, "Zachary, I'm very well versed in handling large things." Zac instantly became aroused by her comment and could barely contain the pulsating erection that pitched his thin lifeguard swim shorts like a tent.

The drive to the city pool from Melany's house was six-minutes, even with heavy traffic, which was a rarity in Weatherford during the summer months—that is unless the city was working on the roads. Exactly halfway to the pool stood a McDonald's on the east side of Main Street.

Seeing the bright yellow arches from about a mile out, Double piped up from the backseat, "Oh, shit, ya'll mind if we hit up some Mickey-D's breakfast?"

Jax quickly yelled, "Hell, yeah—Mel, take us to the arches. I could tear up a sausage biscuit. Nice call, Kool-Aid. I guess being hungry all the time does pay off."

Double took one look at Jax and punched him square in the chest as hard as he could for his comment.

"Ok," gasping for air and holding his arms up in defense. "That's the line, won't cross it again. Noted," Jax said, putting his left hand on his pain-stricken chest.

Melany heard the thud of Double's punch after Jax's comment and asked, "Why do you always have to be an asshole, Jax?"

In his defense, Jax protested, "Mel, I'm not an asshole, I'm quick-witted and I tell the truth. If that hurts your feelings, tough shit; at least I'm honest. Go ahead try me, ask me anything," Jax stated confidently.

Melany couldn't resist the temptation, "Alright, Leesh called me last night and—"

"Fuck that, Mel, that's some shady shit!" Jax stated, becoming defensive.

Zac looked back at Jax and Double turned to his left, doing the same. The two of them shared a baffled looked. The thoughts of what possibly happened between Jax and Alicia took up residence in their minds. Surely, if there were news, Jax would have shared it already with Zac, so why was he being so defensive? Zac could not suppress his curiosity. "What the fuck happened with you and Leesh?"

Jax turned and looked out his window, hoping to get lost in the scenery of Main Street, "Nothing happened, that's what happened," he stated as he drew a penis on his window after the air from his voice fogged it up. Melany knew she had struck a nerve. However, had no clue as to why he took such offense. It didn't' matter. Getting the best of Jax was a rarity, so she indulged in what she considered a victory; she even gave herself a high-five.

Zac was not only confused, but he was also becoming upset from his best friend holding out on him, "Dude, you didn't tell me you were with Leesh last night," Zac stated, feeling offended. "I'll tell you about it later," Jax replied, still looking like a sad puppy staring out of the window.

Double threw his arms up into the air, displeased, and stated, "I suppose I'm going to be left in the dark yet again. Ain't that a motherfucker! A black man being left in the dark, that's why you crackers never see me, how you supposed to see a black man in the dark?"

Jax turned to his right and said, "Paint traffic cones on your titties."

Everyone in the boat cracked up, including Double.

The boat rounded the tight driveway that led to the menu screen and voice box at McDonald's with Melany hugging the left curb. A woman's voice came over the voice box, greeted them and ask if she could take their order. The boat descended the second Double heard the lady ask if she could take their order. Now standing, leaving only his legs in the car as the top of his torso rested out of the sunroof, he roared, "Yeah, I want two sausage biscuits with cheese, a large Coke, and a hash brown with some grape jelly!"

Melany, Zac, and Jax had never seen Double in this form. "What the hell was in that weed you smoked?" Melany queried.

Zac retrieved his sack and smelt it. "Smells normal to me. He must have smoked more because of his large diaphragm," Zac said with a shit grin.

Jax leaned over and looked through what little space was remaining of the sunroof and said, "Double, you do realize you could have allowed Mel to place your order, right?"

Double, now trying to wiggle his way back into the backseat said, "Sorry, guys. I get excited."

Melany looked up and questioned, "You get excited about

McDonald's breakfast?"

Double, still not able to free himself from clinches of the sunroof, said, "Doesn't everyone? They're the best!" The three of them shook their heads in disbelief and finished their order. Zac took a sausage biscuit and a Coke to which Jax added, "Make that two." Melany finished the order and added a small coffee for herself.

A loud thug vibrated through the roof of the boat, "Um, guys, I think I'm really stuck," Double stated, trembling.

Melany smiled at Zac and Jax as they pulled up to the second window to retrieve their order, with Double still halfway out of the boat.

The woman that placed their order didn't say a word as the boat pulled up to the window with Double still struggling to retreat inside. She wore a *what-the-fuck look* on her face.

All Double could do was smile and wave.

CHAPTER 4

PUSSY WAD

When they arrived at the city pool north of the Morrison Community Park, Zac and Jax had to forcefully pull Double from his confinement. It wasn't easy, but with some force and a few scrapes on his back and stomach, Double was freed after riding the last three miles as a roof ornament. Besides Double reenacting Michael J. Fox' character in *Teen Wolf* riding atop the vehicle, the day seemed like any other. It was a warm 76 degrees outside, and since the boat wasn't in motion, Zac threw in the Beastie Boys' new album, "Ill Communication," turned the volume up, and met the others outside in the parking lot for a traditional hacky-sack session.

Looking over at Zac, Melany pointed to her left wrist, silently asking Zac what time he had. "It's 7:23. Why—what's up?" Zac questioned as he retrieved his hacky-sack decorated with a black marijuana leaf from his backpack and tossed it over to Jax.

"Where you gotta be, Mel?" Jax asked. I know the head lifeguard is supposed to be all punctual an' shit, but you got 37 more minutes.

Really doubt Ms. Cleveland is gonna fire you because you didn't open the pool 15 minutes early, ya know."

Melany lost it and lit into Jax, almost shouting, "At least I have ambition, and think about more than getting laid and high like your lame ass."

Zac and Double were leaning back on the boat, watching the show.

"I'm sorry I have goals, Jax, you dumbass! Maybe if you and Leesh—"

Jax stopped her in her tracks before she could divulge any information.

Zac and Double were passively amused by the situation to begin with, but now they were leaned forward and whispering to each other, *"What the fuck happened with Leesh?"*

Jax jogged up the walkway near the only entrance to the pool where Melany stood. "Mel, I'm sorry. I was only giving you shit, promise I won't do it again," he said.

Zac looked over at Double again. "Did he apologize?"

"That man bitched out, that's what he did," Double answered.

Melany looked at Jax oddly, for Jax never, under any circumstance backed down or conceded a fight, so she gladly accepted his apology. She then turned around and unlocked the gate of the pool so she could get things ready for the day.

Jax turned around when Melany reached the gate and began walking back toward Zac and Double.

Zac could not hold back, "You have less than a second to tell me what the fuck is going on!"

Jax patted Zac with his left hand, "Alright man, keep it down, I'll tell you in the breakroom."

Zac bent over to extinguish the cigarette he was smoking.

"Shit, man, let me hit that before you put it out," Jax said, reaching for the cigarette.

Melany was putting out the tables and inserting umbrellas into the small circular center holes to provide shade for the patrons. This usually meant Zac, Jax, and Double had 10 minutes before their official workday began.

Zac reached into the glovebox of the boat and retrieved a plastic holder containing: Clear Eyes, Cool Water Cologne, and hand-wipes. Zac placed drops in each eye without missing a beat, then he handed the bottle to Jax who, in turn, gave it to Double. Next, Zac sprayed his neck and shirt with the cologne, then wiped the resin stains off his fingertips with the wipes. As the three of them removed all evidence of smoking, Melany yelled from poolside, "Are you guys going to work at all today!?" They acted as if she was not even there, put the container back in the glovebox and resumed their hacky-sack game. The boys kicked around the hacky-sack for about five more minutes, each of them trying to invent some sick trick they could showcase at a future party. If one had to choose which of the three were the best hacker, Zac would win hands-down, purely on his footwork alone. Like the piano he had played soccer since he was six and was a shoe-in to make All-State this year, which really helped in the game of hacky-sack.

The bag landed next to Jax's left foot when he noticed he had a hole in his black and white checkered slip-on Vans. "Dude, we should skip out of work at lunch today and hit up the hole," he said.

He was instantly greeted with a choir of, "Hell yes!"

The hole was as it sounded: a hole. However, this particular hole was a water-filled hole out on Paul Colin's land, a dear friend to Zac, Jax, and Double. Those that were friends with Paul had unlimited access to the hole, as long as they could find it. It was the preferred place to chill in the summer for high school, and some junior college, students because they could jump off small cliffs, swim, drink beer, and smoke weed, with little to no risk of being caught by law enforcement. What made it difficult to find were the trees that provided it protection. Massive oaks that easily stood 20 feet tall and stretched for what seemed miles. If you weren't a regular, you'd bet your ass you would be driving and walking around unknown terrain until you found someone that knew the location, or you got lucky as hell.

Double was the first to leave the group and head to clock-in for the day. He wasn't a lifeguard; he ran the snack bar. A perfect fit for a kid who loved junk food and enjoyed looking at hot girls in bikinis. "Alright, fellas, I'll catch you on the flipside, I have to go open the bar before Mrs. Cleveland shows up," Double stated. After giving both Zac and Jax the secret handshake they'd made up in elementary school, Double made his way up to the pool. As Double faded into the distance, Zac looked over at Jax with a puzzled look on his face. "Did he refer to Ms. Cleveland as Mrs.?" Zac inquired.

Jax quickly replied, "He did, probably out of habit, bro. Her divorce has only been final for about a month and a half."

Zac and Jax were about ready to head into the lifeguard breakroom to clock-in for the day as well. Zac stood in front of the boat looking back at Jax who was closing his trunk after retrieving his backpack. Coming into view and making a right turn into the parking lot, Zac noticed a red 1993 Ford Probe: Alicia Armstrong's vehicle. "And what would you do if she walked in here?" Zac said, trying to impersonate Doc Holiday, cringing a bit as he remembered Rick doing the same earlier that morning.

"Who?" Jax replied.

"You know damn well who," Zac said smiling, as he watched Alicia enter the parking lot. Jax gazed over his left shoulder to see what the hell Zac was talking about. "Mother-Fucker!" Jax shouted as he bolted for the front of the boat, grabbed Zac by his t-shirt and took cover behind the front passenger wheel, observing from over the hood as Alicia parked.

Alicia opened her car door, got out and headed inside to the pool for her shift, not even noticing Zac and Jax were hiding on the passenger side of the boat, watching her every move. She was wearing almost the exact same thing as Melany: her red one-piece lifeguard bathing suit, black Umbro shorts, tan Doc Martin sandals, and white Ray-Ban sunglasses. In Zac's eyes, Alicia was the second hottest girl in school—second to Melany. Everyone called her Leesh for short. Her body was fit and tan, which complemented her long, lean legs as she stood almost 5' 10" with long, golden-blonde hair that brushed her ass. Jax had always had a thing for Alicia, but he would never admit it. However, Zac and everyone else for that matter, knew he had a thing for her. Not only because she was hot, but because she could play the bass like Flea from Red Hot Chili Peppers, and she'd performed with them in the talent show.

Zac and Jax followed Alicia with their eyes until she disappeared into the entrance of the city pool. "Hell with the breakroom, man—what happened between you two?" Zac demanded an answer.

Jax looked at him, knowing he wasn't going anywhere until he spilled whatever he was withholding.

"Can you keep a secret?" Jax questioned.

Zac looked at him as if he were joking.

"My bad, dumb question," Jax whispered and went on to tell Zac about his encounter with Alicia the night before. Informing him that after he and Zac split up at Sonic, he'd bumped into her, and she'd invited him over to her house because her folks had gone out to dinner and a movie.

Jax said he was like, "Hell-mother-fucking-yeah—I'm about to get some ass!" So he followed her to her house. When they got inside, she was an animal: attacking him like those girls in the pornos Jax's old man hid in the top of his closet. As she was groping the shit out of him, she led Jax into her living room and pushed him onto her couch. "Stay here," she said, disappearing into another room for about three or four minutes. At the time, the anticipation was killing Jax as he told Zac, "Bro, my cock was throbbing because she made it so fucking hard." When she finally returned, she was butt-naked and holding two lubed-up ping pong balls, a yellow one in her right hand and a white one in her left. Right away I was like, What the shit!? I didn't want to play ping pong; I wanted to hit that." When she got to where Jax was sitting on the couch, she threw her long, tan, sexy, right leg on the left arm of it. Without warning, her well-groomed vagina was, no shit, like two inches from his face. In Jax's mind, he was like, "This is awesome," but he had no clue as to why she was holding those ping pong balls. Then, before Jax could do anything, she said, "Watch this."

Zac knew anytime someone said, "Watch this," some weird shit was about to go down, and Zac loved bizarre shit. He listened intently.

Jax went on to tell Zac that Alicia shoved the yellow ping pong ball up her snatch, quickly following it with the white one.

Zac's eyes were as big as the bottom of a Pepsi can; he couldn't believe his ears. "Are you shitting me, dude!?" Zac was eager to hear all the juicy details: literally.

"Z, that's not the end of it." Jax continued to explain…Alicia looked down at Jax with a crazy ass look on her face and questioned, "You ready?" as she pointed down to her dripping wet vagina.

Jax told Zac he never claimed to be a smart man, but the second she asked, "You ready?" Jax knew he was about to witness something that would forever take up residence in his brain. As Jax was staring at her beautiful, wet vagina, she shot the yellow ping pong ball out, and it hit him in the eye. Jax was like, "What the fuck," and looked up at her, holding his right eye, but at that same moment, the white ball flew out of her vagina, hitting him in the mouth.

Zac sat there in disbelief. "She flipped them around inside her?" he asked, as he began laughing hysterically. Zac added, "Now *that's* some pussy control."

Jax replied, "Z, you're missing the fucking point, the bitch hit me in the mouth with a pussy wad!"

Zac instantly began cry-laughing, questioning, "What did you do?"

Jax told him he threw-up on her carpet, not her pussy carpet, her living room floor carpet and bolted out of her house.

Zac, still laughing uncontrollably, thought Jax's story had concluded and said, "One would think witnessing something so farfetched would be a turn-on."

Jax replied, "Maybe if the pussy wad didn't hit me in the damn mouth, I would have still wanted to hit that, but I fucking puked, dude." Jax asked Zac, "How the hell am I supposed to explain some shit like that, bro?"

Hoping Zac would have some enlightening advice for his distressed friend, he continued to laugh at Jax's self-perceived misfortune. Finally, Zac said, "Tell everyone the truth, man—you were about to get some ass, but she started spitting pussy wads at you."

Jax chuckled and gave him a crisp high-five.

"By the way, how did those titties look without a bathing suit?" Zac probed.

"Fuck off, Z, there are some things a gentleman never shares!" Jax exclaimed.

Zac stood up and helped Jax to his feet, "Come on, man, we have to clock-in and get to our stations; I'll try to paddle her away if I see her coming near you," Zac said with tears in his eyes.

"Fuck you, Z!"

As the morning passed and the hot Oklahoma sun beat down on the patrons at the city pool, Zac started coming down from his high and noticed Jax was too. It was almost 10:30 when Zac ran into Luke as he moved to Station 3 on the south end of the pool. He and Luke chatted briefly, and Luke asked if Zac wanted to head out to the couch and blaze a joint on his next break. Not particularly interested in rolling solo with Luke, Zac told him that Jax and Double would more than likely come along as well if that was cool. Luke showed no objection. The couch was just that, a couch. A few months back, Double's parents purchased new furniture and were planning on discarding their old sofa and loveseat. Instead of allowing his parents to trash their old stuff, Zac, Double, Jax, and Paul decided to haul one of the couches out to the country where they frequently partied when not doing so on Paul's farm. Now that area is commonly referred to as "the couch."

Zac stepped down from Station 3 and walked over to the snack bar to see if Double was interested in a journey out to the couch. "What up, big man?" Zac asked Double as he stepped under the overhang that shaded two snack bars counter.

"Busy as a mother-fucker, Z. Jill called in sick today, so I'm rolling solo, and these little bastards are some needy-ass-bitches," Double replied, referring to all the kids champing at the bit to get their hands on some soda and candy. "What's up with you?"

"Trying not to fry in this damn sun, man. It's already 90 degrees out here, and it isn't even noon. Anyway, so you're out on a couch trip then?" Zac added. There was no way Double could leave, the pool was packed with kids, making it impossible for him to escape. "Yeah, man, these little bastards won't stop coming up here wanting shit." Double looked frustrated.

Zac and Double exchanged their usual handshake, and Zac headed over to Jax who was telling two kids who looked about 9-years-old to stop running—a routine occurrence with little kids at the pool.

Zac approached Jax. He could see he was pissed. Jax was not a big fan of children, especially those that always broke the rules at the pool.

"Z, I swear to God, one day I'm going to bend these damn kids over my knee and open a can of whoop-ass on them," Jax stated as the two boys he'd disciplined walked off.

"Man, stop acting like you're a badass—you're not going to hit a damn kid," Zac said.

"The fuck I won't! Those sons-of-a-bitches need to recognize my authority. I have a whistle. A red one!" Jax said.

Zac laughed and asked, "Hey, Luke wants you and me to join him out on the couch to blaze. Double can't go, he's solo today—you down?" Jax looked at Zac as if he even had to ask. "I swear, Z, you ask the stupidest questions. I really question whether or not you got anything going on upstairs sometimes. I bet that fine-ass mom of yours dropped you on that big ass melon of yours when you were a kid," Jax said laughing.

"Well, let's go then, mother-fucker. Mel is going to cover for us with the other guards," Zac said.

Driving out to the couch in Luke's LTD, the three of them listened to a radio station out of Oklahoma City that played nothing but rock n' roll and alternative music. The DJ's voice echoed out of the speakers,

"This is the Catman on your favorite station in the burbs, 97.3 the FOXX. Right now, I'm going to give lucky caller 94 an entry to win 4 tickets to the concert of the century: Woodstock '94. Which is being held next weekend in New York. Airfare and everything you will need for 3 more days of Peace, Love, and Music will be given to one lucky listener and 3 of their friends tomorrow at 5 p.m. Be sure you continue to listen for your shot at an entry every hour on the hour until then for your chance to win. As for now, I'm going to get all you hippies out there in the mood to rock by playing a song from one of Woodstock 69's top performers, and, as an added bonus, I'll give the first caller that can correctly name which one of the days this performer played at Woodstock '69 a free t-shirt. With that, here's Joe Cocker and The Grease Band's, "With a Little Help from My Friends."

They drove out to the couch, down a long dusty road. Zac, Jax, and Luke were utterly hypnotized by *Joe Cockers* vocals as they did not say a word to each other until the song concluded, which was about the time they arrived at the couch. They usually associated the hit song with TV show *The Wonder Years;* however, on this drive, as they gazed out of the windows staring upon the beautiful countryside Oklahoma had to offer, Zac couldn't help but recall watching the movie *Woodstock* with his uncle; a movie they had watched together numerous times over the years. The original Woodstock immortalized Jimmy Hendrix for his rendition of "The Star Spangled Banner," but, to Zac, Joe Cocker stole the show with his soul-bearing, psychedelic, performance. Zac closed his eyes and began to imagine he was the balding long-haired hippy that could briefly be seen watching Joe and his band perform the hit song. He could see Joe standing there, wearing his tie-dye t-shirt, bellbottom jeans, and sea-blue boots with white stars on them as he jammed on what's believed to be the first "air guitar." It might have been what the DJ said, "Three more days of Peace, Love, and Music," but Zac couldn't stop thinking what it might have been like had he been a young man in that era. He didn't share his thoughts with Jax or Luke. It was a moment that gave him chills, and he knew they wouldn't do anything but tease on him if he shared these thoughts.

The couch was located about eight miles east of Weatherford and protected by the closest thing you could call a forest in the flatlands of Oklahoma: about twenty or so trees in the middle of the county—much like Paul's family's land. Nobody knew whose property it was on, but it was in the middle of nowhere and had never been tampered with in the almost year since Zac and his crew had staked the ground as their own; much like the 1889 Oklahoma Land Rush. Luke began to remove the large weathered green tarp that protected the couch from the harsh Oklahoma weather and set it on the left side before taking a seat. "I saw a commercial for Woodstock '94 on MTV this morning as I was getting ready," Luke stated as he put a joint to his mouth. "I saw that, too," Jax said before adding, "They're having some big contest where the winner gets a tricked-out Winnebago and like five-grand to take them and some friends to the concert."

As their imaginations ran crazy, it was clear that attending Woodstock '94 was monopolizing their thoughts. "I heard on the radio the other day that the *Chili Peppers*, *Aerosmith*, *Cypress Hill*, *Green Day*, *Nine Inch Nails*, and *Metallica* are all going to be playing there," Zac stated with excitement. Zac was a bit like Jax and The Beatles in regard to liking the Red Hot Chili Peppers. They were, by far, his favorite band, and he was yet to see them live.

Jax reached across his body for the joint Luke was passing, adding, "Man, could you imagine being able to attend Woodstock '94? Shit, brothers, that's what dreams are made of!" Deep down, Zac knew it was precisely that, a dream. There was no way in hell Rick would ever allow him to go to New York, let alone go to New York to attend Woodstock '94. He flips out when Zac tells him he's going to Oklahoma City with his friends, which is only about an hour away from Weatherford. Not only that, his family was poor. There was no way he could ever afford to travel that far away from home.

Back at the pool, adult swim was about to begin. Adult swims reserved the last fifteen minutes of every hour for those eighteen and older to be able to swim without kids everywhere. It also provided the lifeguards a short break, as only one lifeguard, not four, were required to be on station during that time. Melany directed the newest lifeguard to take Station 1 on the north side of the pool when she noticed Alicia approaching her with a concerned expression.

"Hey, girl, why the long face?" Melany asked.

Alicia looked around the pool, glancing from left to right, as if she were searching for eavesdroppers. "Hey, Mel, have you by chance spoken with Jax today?" she questioned as expecting to get a negative reply.

Melany hesitated for a second and reached out to her right, stopping a kid that couldn't have been more than eight or nine, as she noticed him running out of the corner of her eye, "Stop running, that is your last warning! If I have to tell you again, you'll have to leave for the rest of the day!" The boy, who was dancing in place because the hot concrete was burning the bottoms of his feet, was clearly embarrassed, and simply replied, "Yes, ma'am," then headed to the snack bar with his two friends as they both pointed and made fun of him. "I'm sorry,

Leesh, what did you ask?"

"I was curious if you talked with Jax at all today," she asked.

"I drove him, Zac, and Mike to work in the boat, but he and Zac went on break with Luke, so it's been a while. Why what's up?" Melany asked.

Alicia, who was now looking down at the ground, almost as if she were trying to avoid eye contact said, "I wanted to chat with him about last night is all."

Melany punched Alicia in her right arm, not to hurt her, it was a gesture of "Oh my God," you won't believe what I'm about to tell you and almost shouted, "Speaking of last night, I have no clue what you were going to tell me regarding Jax, but don't. This morning I was getting ready to tell him that you and I spoke, but before I could tell him I had to get off the phone with you, he interrupted me, like he thought I knew something I shouldn't. He's been hella chill to me ever since."

Alicia, who appeared to be relieved as hell that Melany didn't know about the ping pong story told her, "Yeah, I thought about it as well, and this one should probably stay between Jax and I."

Melany paused and examined Alicia. Her body language wasn't as spunky as it usually was and she had to ask, "Are you crushing on Jax, Leesh?"

Alicia looked as if she were about to deny Melany's best friend intuition. "I was, but after last night, I'm not sure how he feels about me."

Melany scoffed at her, "Girl, if I know one thing about Jax, it's that he needs some time to feel like a player. You know how he thinks he's Snoop Dogg in Beatles attire."

The two shared a quick laugh, knowing damn well that was a spot-on description of Jax.

"I hope you're right. By the way, what were you going to tell me about Z?" Alicia said, trying to shift the focus off of herself. "Oh yeah!" But as Melany opened her mouth to answer, a loud whistle blew, and a herd of kids all cannonballed into the pool, indicating adult swim had concluded. "I'll have to tell you later!" Mel shouted. Her voice echoing as she headed to Station 1 to give the new guard a break.

CHAPTER 5

I WANT TO HOLD YOUR HAND

Melany stepped down from Station 1 after spending 45 minutes watching most of the patrons at the pool cool themselves from the blistering 105 degree Oklahoma heat. She headed to the snack bar to see how Double was handling working alone. Before reaching the bar, she glanced to her left, peering through the chain-link fence, noticing Luke's LTD pulling into the parking lot. "What's up, Mike—you doing alright?" she questioned.

Double looked like an obese man trying to run a mile, gasping for air because of the demands that came from running the only booth that provided refreshments. "Mel, I'm dying here, girl!"

Melany walked around the side of the bar and entered through the side door. "Grab a bottle of water and go sit in the AC for a bit, I'll cover for a while," she demanded.

"Damn, you're cool as a fan girl!" Double replied and grabbed two bottles of water from the cooler before heading to the break room, which happened to be the only room with air conditioning.

Melany could see why Double felt like he was dying, during adult swim, the snack bar was overloaded with kids buying anything from nachos, to popcorn; the line of loitering children was relentless. However, the second the whistle blew, concluding adult swim, the kids in the front of the line, eagerly awaiting to spend their parent's money on the treats of their choice, vanished without a trace. As Zac, Jax, and Luke came through the entrance of the pool they walked right past Mel as she was operating the bar. "How was the couch, boys?" she questioned with a smirk on her face, knowing all three of them were high as hell.

They all approached the counter when they heard the question. "Memorable!" Zac replied.

"Hey, Mel, I think we're going to get burgers before we drop off Kool-Aid, you in?" Jax asked. Mel looked over to Zac almost as if she were looking for his permission to join them, noticing he was unconsciously nodding his head up and down. "Sure, can I invite Leesh?" she probed.

Jax flipped her off and headed to the bathroom, with Luke following, minus the gratuitous gesture.

"I'll take that as a no," Melany yelled.

"Ditto," Zac added.

Melany turned her attention to Zac, "What happened between those two last night?" Mel asked.

Zac, hiding behind his Oakley Sunglasses, couldn't camouflage his perplexed expression, asking, "You mean you don't know?"

Melany said she'd spoken to Alicia on the phone late last night, but before Alicia could divulge any information, Melany's father had asked her to help him dry off Scarlett, her tan and white English Bulldog because he'd given the 50-pound muscle beast her weekly bath.

Zac smiled, thinking to himself how funny the entire situation was—even better, how he could use this newly discovered information to mess with Jax.

"So, what actually happened with them, do you know?" Melany inquired.

Zac went with the first thing that popped into his head, "They played ping-pong."

Melany tilted her head, confused, looking like Scarlett when she heard a strange noise, turning her head a bit to the right, bright-eyed with curiosity.

Zac thought the look on Melany's face was absolutely adorable. "That's it! He's being a little bitch because they played ping-pong? I know that girl has skills with the paddle, but she must have really handed him an ass-whooping!"

Zac was tearing up from the extreme effort required to prevent from doubling over with uncontrollable laughter. "I thought the same. So, lunch then?" Zac asked as he stepped back, knowing he had to get to his station.

"Of course, I'll meet you guys at the boat, and without Leesh, I suppose," Melany added with a smile.

After the 11 o'clock hour passed, Melany turned over snack bar duties to the newest guard arriving for the lunch hour, then met Zac, Jax, and Double in the parking lot. They all took their places: Jax driving, Double sitting shotgun, and Melany and Zac comfortably in the spacious back seat. This afternoon, Jax did the unexpected. After turning the ignition and bringing the classic automobile to life, the crew heard sounds blaring through the speakers that none of them had ever heard while the boat was setting sail. The song "Insane in the Membrane" by Cypress Hill blessed their ears; instantly sending them into a dancing frenzy in their seats. "Screw it, everything else about this day has been insane, might-as-well keep the shit going!" Jax exclaimed. Everyone shouted, "Hellz Yeah!" and the boat set out on its course so they could all grab a burger, fries, and a Route-44 cherry vanilla cola. The preferred meal for all parties, except for Melany, she favored their cherry lime-aids.

With their meals almost consumed, the song "I Want to Get High" began to play on Jax's CD player as they sat in parking slot number five. It was one of the few stalls that possessed enough shade to keep the boat cool without using the AC as they enjoyed their food. Hearing the song, Jax opened the ashtray directly under the CD player and retrieved a joint. "What do you say, Mel, you down?" Jax asked, sliding the joint under his nose, smelling the sweet skunky aroma it emanated.

"What the hell, the workday is almost over, and I don't think Ms. Cleveland is going to be at the pool this afternoon," Melany said with her perfect smile.

Jax, Double, and Zac all shared the same look of shock and awe. The music, the moment, must have gotten the best of her; she never smoked while on duty. Never!

"You don't *think*, or you *know,* she's not going to be there this afternoon?" Zac inquired, using air quotes. Zac was excited to smoke with Melany while working; however, he was also concerned. The last thing in the world he ever wanted was for her get in trouble and possibly jeopardize her employment.

"I don't think she is. She mentioned something about taking her son to the dentist this afternoon," Melany said.

Double held his left hand up behind his head, offering Melany a high-five while adding, "You go with your badass self, Mel!"

While hesitant, Jax and Zac both decided to finish the workday out to help pay tribute to Melany's first day of being stoned at work. Double too wanted to share in the momentous occasion with his best friends; however, he only worked half days, as he took college courses at the local junior college during the summer afternoons and couldn't ditch class. The four of them continued to enjoy the hypnotic flow of Cypress Hill's lyrics as they smoked out while listening to the rap Gods. While doing so, Zac noticed a look in Melany's eyes he had never seen before. She sat relaxed and free-willed as she pulled her dark, curly hair out of its ponytail and let it flow freely in the wind that the open window provided as they sailed across town. It was like she didn't have a care in the world and as she looked over at Zac, nibbling on her bottom lip, watching him hit the joint, he was overcome with the feeling that in some odd way she was trying to flirt with him. He knew such thoughts were futile, though. She was by far the hottest, smartest, most talented girl in Weatherford. While he desperately wanted to be her boyfriend, he knew there was no way in hell she saw him as anything other than a friend.

Suddenly the boat came to a screeching halt in front of Double's parents' mansion. "What are we doing?" Zac questioned, still mesmerized by Melany's beauty and his thoughts of them together.

Everyone glared at him oddly, "The same thing we do every day, dip-shit, dropping Kool-Aid off so he can get his education on," Jax said as he abruptly felt Double's massive right hook land square in his chest yet again. "I warned you about that Kool-Aid shit, you caucasian mother-fucker!" Double said.

Zac tried to snap out of it and orientate himself with his location; he had merely lost track of his surroundings, a frequent occurrence for him in the presence of the only girl he had ever truly loved.

Double exited the boat, and, as usual, the right side of the vessel immediately raised from the relief of his departure. Exhaling a deep breath, probably from the effort it took to lift himself from the boat, Double asked, "We doing a pregame before Luke's party tonight?" It was a fair question, as that was a longstanding tradition the group had participated in before showing up to every gathering or event they had ever attended since junior high. He waited for what seemed like five minutes, only to receive three blank expressions on the faces of three very high 18-year-olds. Melany, however, was wearing her stare while slurping on the red straw of her cherry lime-aid with her head slightly cocked to the side.

Double smirked and added, "Lightweights!"

Jax, Melany, and Zac laughed at his remark. "All right then, page me later and let me know what's up," Double shut the car door and turned toward his house.

Jax was never in favor of returning to work after lunch. Especially because Melany usually hooked everyone up on their timecards, ensuring they all got paid, even in their absence from work. Jax's longstanding mantra was, "Why the hell go back if I can get paid to do the shit I want to do." It made perfect sense; yet, it was apparent Zac wanted to be around Melany, particularly with her being high at work. It was odd, but there was something about the way she allowed herself to be carefree while stoned that captured his imagination, and he wasn't going to miss this workday for the world. Besides, it was his birthday, and he figured he could do whatever the he wanted, and Jax knew this about his best friend. Jax was only upset because his idea about going to the hole after lunch wouldn't happen today.

There were occasions Jax did enjoy returning to work after lunch; however, those days were reserved for when Mrs. Baker, Luke's mom, was sunbathing poolside. Luke's mom was ridiculously beautiful. She had a golden tan, legs up to her armpits, amazing fake tits that almost fell out of her swimsuit, and a body that showed zero evidence of ever having given birth to two boys, let alone that she was in her mid-40's. Mrs. Baker also taught senior English, all of which Zac and his crew would be attending in the upcoming school year. Jax always told people that he was like Van Halen when it came to Mrs. Baker, "Hot For Teacher." Not everyone got the joke, but Zac did, as did Luke. Luke hated the fact that all his friends wanted to have sex with his mom. Zac believed that was the reason Luke was always giving Jax a hard time about girls, he knew no one was more obsessed with his mom. Jax would even go as far as telling Luke he couldn't wait to get some one-on-one tutelage from his mom next year, he'd also add that he might be able to teach *her* a thing or two as well.

Upon returning to the pool, Jax, Melany, and Zac noticed they had about fifteen minutes until their lunch break concluded, so the three of them decided to hangout in the breakroom to relax before taking their stations and relieving the other lifeguards waiting to take their lunch breaks. The breakroom was pretty simple, however, it had the distinct smell of chlorine and moldy towels. There was a water fountain on the left side next to a small refrigerator, a round table in the center with five chairs pushed under it; all of which resembled the kind of setup one would find in an elementary school classroom, and one window that opened up to the parking lot. On the far right, there was a small office with a massive brown door that was always propped open by a block of wood, leaving the office opened a crack, allowing in cool air from the air conditioner. Inside the office was a small desk with an old metal chair, and an antique gray metal filing cabinet that stood about five feet high with four drawers and a whiteboard that hung on the wall.

Ms. Cleveland utilized the whiteboard to post reminders that pertained to her staff, something each lifeguard reviewed both at the beginning and end of the day. The only two people who ever really utilized the office were Ms. Cleveland and Melany, nobody else had a reason to go in there, except to look at the board for any new postings. Even Ms. Cleveland rarely spent time there during duty hours.

Zac had leaned over the water fountain to get a drink when he heard Jax's voice yell out behind him, "Aren't you guys fucking stoned? That shit must have been laced, 'cause I'm seriously fucked up!" Zac laughed, preventing him from swallowing his drink. "Dude, you made the water come out my nose." Zac grinned while trying to dry the water dripping from his chin, which made Melany laugh hysterically. The laughter in the room briefly drowned out the sound of an old metal chair grinding across the concrete floor. However, the noise eventually captured Melany and Zac's attention as their eyes locked on to the brown door of the office. An office they had believed to be empty. Without warning, the sizeable door flew open with ungodly velocity, "Who said that!" Ms. Cleveland demanded to know as she exited the office, scaring the living shit out of Zac and Melany. Though Ms. Cleveland had to know it was Zac or Jax, since it was the voice of a male that she'd heard, and they were the only two males in the room.

Melany and Zac stood motionless, hearts pounding, like deer in headlights about to be struck by a semi-truck flying down the highway. Jax looked up, his back toward the office, and without hesitation said, "I did, mother-fucker! I'm blown out of my mind right now." It was apparent Jax had no clue it was Ms. Cleveland doing the inquiring. She stood directly behind him, bright-red, vain-popping anger was surging through her 5' 3" frame. She was wearing the required lifeguard uniform, a red one-piece swimsuit and matching shorts, both of which matched the shade of her pissed-off face. Still sitting and peering over his right shoulder, Jax saw her, then looked over at Zac and Mel and smiled at them before returning his attention to their angry leader. "Damn, Ms. Cleveland, I thought you were at an appointment," he stated with a laugh. It took every ounce of bearing Melany and Zac possessed not to laugh as the weed giggles were screaming to come out and join the party.

Ms. Cleveland glanced over at Melany and Zac with a piercing squint, looking for any evidence that they too had smoked pot during their lunch hour. "Are you two high as well!? Is this what kind of show you run while I'm not around, Melany!" Ms. Cleveland stated as she continued her interrogation.

Jax quickly noticed Melany was shaking at the knees and had no clue what to do as she stood there frozen, hoping something smart would roll off his tongue, allowing her to escape this predicament. Jax quickly pushed his chair out from under the table and stood stating, "Why are you asking if they're high? I'm the one that said I was fucked up," he said, hoping to turn Ms. Cleveland's attention toward him.

Ms. Cleveland sneered, "Jax, you asked, *Aren't you guys fucking stoned?* meaning plural, as in more than just you! So again, who else in here is high right now?" Ms. Cleveland asked, demanding an answer. Jax quickly replied in protest, "Damn, woman, it was me; they weren't with me. I blazed by myself." Still, in disbelief and reaching levels of frustration none of them had ever witnessed, Ms. Cleveland added, "I know you all went to lunch together, you always do!" Her voice was now hitting ranges that suggested shit was getting real, fast!

Zac noticed Jax was drawing a blank, a rarity in these situations, so he took the lead, praying to get Melany out of this predicament. He wasn't worried about himself or Jax, only her. He took a step toward his boss and said, "Ms. Cleveland, I took Jax's car today. Double, I mean, Mike, and Mel went with me to Sonic for lunch. Jax said he had to meet someone at the park next door during lunch, so he gave me his keys."

Ms. Cleveland pointed fiercely toward the exit, "Melany, Zac, get to your stations right now and relieve the other guards. Jax, get your ass in my office, now!" she demanded.

Melany and Zac, while almost crapping their suits, sprinted out of the breakroom and shut the door behind them as fast as they could. Hoping they had dodged a bullet and that Jax didn't get the cops called on him, or worse, his father. For he would surely kick the crap out of him.

Ms. Cleveland wasted zero time, "What the hell were you thinking, Jax, you're a Goddamn lifeguard for Christ's sake! Do you have any clue what that means?" She didn't give him a chance to answer, "It means you're in charge of the safety and wellbeing of everyone that walks through the gates of this establishment, and lives are, literally, at stake. Don't you take that seriously?" she questioned, impatiently awaiting his response.

"You want me to be honest?" Jax asked.

The veins in Ms. Cleveland's forehead were now bulging as they formed the shape of a V. "No, Jax, lie to me," she said, sarcastically.

Jax looked her in the eyes, "Not really, it's a job," he stated with zero emotion. It was as if he had ice running through his body, he was as cool as the Fonz from the show The Happy Days. There he stood, being ripped a new one by his superior and he appeared as calm as a kid ordering a Happy Meal at McDonald's.

"Just a job! What do you think would happen if some kid were to drown while you were on your station and you were too high to notice—what then, Jax?"

Jax replied, "I'm sure one of the other lifeguards would notice the kid struggling."

Ms. Cleveland took a step back and was now wearing a dumbfounded look on her face, unable to comprehend the words that exited Jax's month. "Please tell me you're not serious right now," she stated.

Jax continued, "I'm just saying, the other guards are pretty good at what they do, they look out for that sort of thing. "You're really pissed aren't you?" Jax inquired, suggesting he hadn't noticed a damn thing that had transpired in the last five minutes.

Ms. Cleveland didn't even know how to respond, she simply stated, rhetorically, "You think, Jax?"

Melany and Zac partially followed Ms. Cleveland's demands. They did immediately exit the breakroom; however, after shutting the door behind them, both of them put their ears against the metal door, hoping to hear Jax's fate. Melany had her left ear pushed as hard as she could against the door. Zac did the same with his right ear. They stood, hunched over, almost nose to nose, listing. Attempting to make out anything they could, everything just sounded like Charlie Brown's teacher, "Wah Wah Wah."

"Do you think she'll call the cops on him?" Melany asked Zac as she stood almost paralyzed with a paranoid look on her face.

Zac stood up and moved away from the door. "I don't think so, Jax has a gift of getting out of predicaments like this somehow," he stated before telling her about something that happened to Jax and him a while back. A few weeks ago, he and Jax were driving home after smoking out on the couch. They had turned off the dirt road onto Route 66, and Jax ran a stop sign. The same sign that 99.9% of all drivers on that country road ignore, so it was nothing out of the norm. What they didn't realize was the county sheriff deputy's vehicle was parked behind a billboard that Douglas County was in the process of tearing down. The deputy flipped on his lights and pulled them over. Zac was stoned out of his mind, and freaking out, much like Melany did in the breakroom, but multiplied by 100. Zac's hands wouldn't stop shaking he so terrified. Jax parked the boat on the shoulder of road, and the deputy walked up to Jax' side of the vehicle and requested his license and registration. As usual, Jax calmly asked, "What's the problem, officer?" While Zac sat fumbling through the glovebox looking for Jax' credentials. As he did so, he accidentally dropped the plastic box that contained the Clear Eyes, Cool Water Cologne, and hand-wipes on the floorboard. Knowing damn well the cop saw it, Zac kept his head down, avoiding eye contact at all cost.

Finally, Zac found the paperwork and handed it to Jax. Zac knew the deputy could see him shaking and thought for sure he'd ask what the contents in the plastic container were for. Zac could feel the deputy looking into his soul, his heartbeat raced. Zac's body temperature rose, and he began to get all sweaty, bottom line: he was having a panic attack. Jax took notice, but he smoothly grabbed the papers from Zac's sweaty hand and gave him a wink. It was as if he was telling Zac to, "Watch this," again preparing Zac for some weird shit.

The deputy informed Jax he had pulled him over because he had failed to come to a complete stop back at the stop sign before getting on the highway. Zac told Melany, "I shit you not," Jax looked him in the eye and said to the deputy, "My bad, officer. I thought the stop signs with the white rings around them were optional." Zac recalled thinking, "What the fuck—who the hell comes up with that kind of shit!?" However, the deputy looked back at Jax like he couldn't believe this kid had the stones to say that to him. He glanced over at Jax's license and registration and told them to sit tight as he made his way back to his vehicle. Zac glanced at Jax with a crazy look, while Jax sat patiently, smiling and drumming on his steering wheel, like this was an everyday occurrence. I was freaking out and told Jax that Rick was going to kick my ass. Jax said, "Calm down, Z, I got this."

After a few minutes, they watched the deputy in the rearview mirror as he strolled back to the boat wearing a shit-eating grin on his face. Zac knew that was it, they were going to be taken into custody for sure. The deputy reached out and handed Jax a driver's manual stating, "Son, that white ring bit was the funniest damn thing I've ever heard in my twelve years on the force. Here are your documents; and by-the-way, the stop signs with the white rings around them are not optional: you have to come to a complete stop at those as you would all stop signs. Take a look in that manual when you get a chance. Now it doesn't mention white rings, but it does tell you what to do when approaching a stop sign."

Jax nodded and said, "I'll keep that in mind from now on."

The deputy began to return to his car but quickly turned back toward Jax and said, "Oh yeah, one more thing…Tell your buddy there to chill-out, freaking out like that under pressure is a dead giveaway you two were smoking weed out in the country."

Zac's jaw hit the floor, and Jax replied, "I will, thanks, man!"

The deputy returned to his vehicle and proceeded to drive down the road.

Jax followed suit, as if nothing had happened.

While driving off, Jax looked over at Zac, back-handed him in the chest with his right hand and said, "I told you I had that shit, brother!" Zac had never questioned his skills since.

Melany looked at Zac with confusion.

"What?" Zac asked.

"There are stop signs that don't have white rings around them?" she questioned.

Zac had never put much thought into it. "I have no idea," he stated with a shrug.

Both of them smiled and simultaneously said, "Fucking Jax."

Jax knew his time as a lifeguard was about to abruptly end, so he did what Jax did best, he attempted to turn a crappy situation into something he could benefit from. This was a gift that couldn't be taught, it was a blessing from God and anyone that knew him well understood this was a gift he possessed. He was a verbal ninja, and always got what his heart desired. He took a step toward Ms. Cleveland flexing the muscles in his jaw and tightening his pecks, and abs then explained, "I know you're pissed, and trust me, you have every right to be. I'm certain I would be as well if the shoe were on the other foot, but I have to tell you, Racheal, you're so fucking hot when you're pissed."

Ms. Cleveland replied with a simple, "What?" as if she didn't understand Jax statement.

He moved closer toward her, standing close enough he could feel her breath becoming heavier.

"Jax, what are you doing?" she questioned, knowing she already knew the answer.

He grabbed her with his muscular right arm, wrapped it around her waist and pulled her against his body. She could feel his hard cock grinding into her above her pelvic area, and it made her instantly aroused. She felt herself getting wet through her thin bathing suit. It was a feeling she hadn't experienced since before her divorce. Jax looked down at her smiling, as he towered a good eight inches above her. She slowly looked up at him, as he pulled her face closer to his, leaned his head to the right, and gently kissed her soft, moist lips; a gesture she returned.

"Wait, we can't do this, you work for me, and you're way too young!" she exclaimed as she tried to escape his grasp.

Jax smiled again then replied, "I'm 18, and I quit."

She stared into his eyes as anger was replaced with unwavering lust. Moving both of her hands, placing one on each of his cheeks she kissed him passionately; their tongues moved in perfect harmony, arousing both of them immensely. Jax ran his hands downward, placing them on her tight ass and lifted her off the ground as she wrapped her tan, athletically toned legs around his waist, like a python smothering its prey. Stumbling, he carried her into her office, laid her down on top of the desk and aggressively slid all the contents that resided on it crashing to the floor.

Ms. Cleveland quickly began to untie Jax swimming trunks as he ripped her shorts off as well. Once they were removed, she pushed him off of her making him stand beside the desk. Rising to her feet, Ms. Cleveland firmly grabbed his rock-hard cock and began stroking it gently. Noticing Jax's eyes rolling back in his head she went to her knees and inserted his dick deep into her mouth, sucking and licking it like a kid wearing ring candy. "Take that shit," Jax said as Ms. Cleveland engulfed every inch of his cock, gagging herself repeatedly. Jax stopped her abruptly and pulled her up, tore off her one-piece swimsuit and flipped her over, face down, on her desk. "Fuck me, you little shit!" she demanded. Jax grabbed a handful of her long brown hair and inserted his pulsating cock into her dripping wet pussy. Thrusting harder and harder, faster and faster.

She did everything in her power to remain quiet, "You fucking like that big cock, huh?" Jax asked as he smacked her right ass cheek.

She couldn't refrain, "I can feel you in my throat!" she screamed, to which Jax smiled. The desk was banging against the brick wall, chipping it every time it struck. "I'm gonna cum!" Jax exclaimed. At that moment, Ms. Cleveland was hitting an orgasm as she had never encountered, "Give it to me!" she demanded. "Holy Hell!" Jax yelled as he orgasmed himself.

Jax grabbed a towel that was hanging on the back of the metal chair and said, "Damn girl, you got some fucking skills, literally." Handing her the towel to clean herself up she replied, "Jax that was amazing. I've never been done anything remotely like that, and I was married for years!" She stood up, and began to get dressed, "You know, my son is sleeping over at his friends' tomorrow night, you're more than welcome to come over for a repeat if you'd like," she stated.

Jax looked at her, paused, then asked, "Racheal, do you know what song of The Beatles was their first to hit number one in the USA?" An odd question she thought, given the timing,

"No, why do you ask that?" she answered perplexed. Jax laughed and replied, "Well, then, there is the answer to your question, no." Jax headed for the exit; however, before leaving, he turned to face her and said, "Racheal, thank you for a memorable summer, and so you know, the song was "I Want to Hold Your Hand." It topped the charts in 1964. Paving the way for the British Invasion." Jax turned toward the door, opened it, and walked out, not saying another word.

CHAPTER 6

LET'S GET A TACO

Back at Zac's apartment, Janis and Rick were meeting up to have lunch together. This was a rare occurrence since Rick usually had a difficult time getting away from work in the middle of the day. They arrived home only seconds apart and greeted each other with a warm kiss in their driveway. That was one thing Zac couldn't fault Rick for. He may not have been the best father-figure in his eyes, but he loved Janis more than anything in the world.

"How's your day going, my love," Janis asked as she walked into the kitchen to get lunch started.

Rick sat at the kitchen table. "It's a little busy, but that's nothing new. How are things at the shop?" Rick asked in return.

Janis went on to explain her day was pretty hectic because Cassy, one of two employees was out with the flu; leaving June, the newest employee, to run things while she stepped out for lunch.

Rick responded, "Make sure they give Cassy plenty of days off, the last thing we need right now is the flu. Besides, I've got a few things

I'm going to need Zac's help with in the upcoming weeks, and I don't need him to get sick on me."

Janis saw this as the perfect opportunity to discuss what she and Zac spoke about at breakfast earlier in the morning. "Speaking of Zachary, I was hoping I could talk to you about your plans for him for the remainder of the summer."

Rick sighed. He recognized this was not going to end well. He knew both Janis and Zac believed he was too hard on the boy. However, he played along, "What is it now?" almost like there was always something when it came to Zac.

Janis stepped to the side of the cupboard, the only obstacle obstructing her from seeing Ricks face, "What is that supposed to mean?" Janis stated in a defensive tone.

Rick thought to himself, *here we go,* then attempted to explain to Janis, "I'm trying to provide the boy with a strong work ethic and morals he'll one day value, Janis. The boy is walking a delicate line, and if he falters, I'm afraid he won't possess what it takes to get back on the right path is all. You've seen the kids he hangs out with, they're trouble, and you know it."

Janis clenched her jaw.

Rick could tell her blood was about to boil.

"Zachary is an amazing young man! He does excellent with his studies and lives by the rules we put in place. I don't believe, for a second, he's falling off any "path." If anything, he's going to get pushed off the right path by you!"

Rick realized she wasn't going to back down; however, he was notorious for not backing down from an argument himself—sometimes taking things a tad bit too far when arguing with Janis. This argument was developing into one of those times. Unable to resisted he added, "I push him? If anything, it will be your damn brother doing the pushing. He has that kid thinking he can follow in his footsteps and make a living going to rock concerts and God knows what kind of festivals. He's turning Zac into a damn hippie for crying out loud!"

If there were one thing Janis would not tolerate, it was someone, regardless of whom, talking negatively about her family, including Rick. "Rick, I'm gonna say this one time, so you better listen very clearly. Jimmy is an extremely talented man, and if our son becomes a fraction of the man Jimmy is, I'll consider our parenting a success."

Rick couldn't let it go, however. "You're kidding me, right—you consider becoming a t-shirt selling pot-head successful?"

She couldn't believe what she heard come out of his mouth. He knew damn well Jimmy cared for people more than anyone else they knew and added, "You think Jimmy only gets high and travels around in a motorhome, city to city watching the Grateful Dead? You might want to take a look in the mirror, mister, before you begin to pass judgment. I can recall a time not so long ago you thought being a hippie was the best thing in the world."

She had a point. Rick had been a "free spirit" in his younger days, but, in his mind, it was merely a phase, not a profession.

"You know, you're right, Janis, I did enjoy that kind of lifestyle, and it was a great time, but then I pulled my head out of my ass and got a real job so I could provide for our family, do you remember that?"

Janis quickly reminded him that Jimmy went to law school and graduated with honors.

Rick couldn't' refrain, though. He viewed Janis' last comment like a slow pitch coming down the middle of the plate, and he was going to swing for the fence. "He went to Berkley! All hippies graduate with honors from Berkley. The first day the professors hand out their syllabus, it states, "Be sure to come to school stoned to graduate with honors!"

Janis glared at him, as if wishing he were a voodoo doll she could stab repeatedly with a sharp object. "You can be such an asshole sometimes, you know that!" she stated as she slammed the cupboard door shut, nearly tearing it from its hinges.

Rick smiled. "Call them as I see them, baby," he replied with a sly smile.

Janis stormed past him. "I can't even look at you right now. I'll grab something to eat on my way back to the store. By the way, don't forget we are entertaining Zachary's "terrible" friends tonight, so set things up by your damn self, and it better be perfect by the time I get home."

Rick tried to reach out for her as she stormed by, "Oh, come on, don't be like that," he protested.

She continued on her way, slamming the front door as hard as she could in frustration.

Rick sat in silence. *The one day I take time off to help out, and I get this shit! And now I even have to make my own damn sandwich,* he thought to himself.

Jax left the breakroom with a smile, shaking his head in disbelief over what had happened. Melany was attending Station 1 when she noticed his exit. Zac was operating the snack bar while the other lifeguards were on their lunch breaks. Melany desperately wanted to step down and find out what was happing with Jax, but there were no other lifeguards available to cover for her at the moment. Jax looked across the pool at her, holding both hands up in the air, implying he was searching for Zac. Melany pointed toward the snack bar. Jax gave her a thumbs-up and made his way to the bar. "*I Feel Fine*!" Jax sang at the top of his lungs as he jumped up on the snack bar counter taking a seat, while simultaneously startling the shit out of Zac who had not seen Jax exit the breakroom. At the time all the kids were swimming, so Zac had been sitting behind the counter, nervously waiting to find out his best friends fate.

Once Zac caught his breath, he questioned, "Dude, what the hell went on in there?"

Jax put his left hand on Zac's right shoulder and said, *"All You Need is Love, Z!"* quoting yet another Beatles song.

Zac looked at him confused at first. Suddenly, Zac's eyes lit up, "No fucking way, you didn't!" Zac stated in utter disbelief.

Jax, wearing his usual big ass smile simply said, "Indeed I did, sir—indeed I did!" Jax went on, "And, Z, that woman has some fucking skills." Jax laughed hysterically.

Zac had to know, "What's so funny?"

"I literally just told Racheal the exact same thing," Jax replied.

Zac laughed and said, "Oh, her name is Racheal now?"

Jax told Zac everything that had happened, not leaving out any of the juicy details.

"So did you get fired?" Zac inquired.

Jax gazed at Zac with the an astonished *don't you know who the fuck I am* kind of look. "Hellz no, I quit before she had a chance to fire me. Ain't no way I'm letting someone fire my ass!" he exclaimed.

Zac shook his head. "You're crazy, man."

Jax turned his head and looked up at the sky. "Some people might call my antics crazy, but I would say—well, crazy, I suppose."

They both cracked up laughing.

Jax hopped off the counter.

"So now what?" Zac asked.

"Well, I suppose this is the end of the pool for me, my friend. Nothing left to conquer here, if you know what I'm saying."

Zac lifted his eyebrows and thought to himself, *he's right, he has literally had sex with every girl that works at the pool, excluding Melany, of course*

Jax and Zac exchanged handshakes, and Jax took two steps toward the pool exit, "Oh, Z, thanks for the save in there by the way. Not too shabby for someone that usually freaks out under pressure."

Zac smiled and added, "What can I say, brother, I've got a pretty good mentor."

"Indeed you do, young grasshopper. I'll pick you guys up at four; I'm Audi-5000, bitches!" Jax exited the pool, as Zac sat behind the counter, still shaking his head and laughing to himself in disbelief that Jax had quit his job and screwed their boss; all in less than 30 minutes.

Lunch had concluded, and Alicia relieved Melany who immediately ran to the snack bar, eager to learn what had happened to Jax. "So, what's the deal?" she asked in a paranoid tone.

Zac wanted to give her all the details; however, he couldn't, he didn't feel it was his place. So he went with, "He quit."

She looked stumped. "That's it. He quit? Did he say anything about Ms. Cleveland busting us, or calling the cops?"

Zac grabbed her hand, hoping to calm her down as he knew she was still high and scared out of her mind, being this was uncharted territory for her. "I don't think Ms. Cleveland wants the fact that she can't seem to control her employees publicly known. I think this one is pretty much a closed case, and don't worry, I don't believe she's going to be asking us any questions about our participation." Zac said, doing his best to help her unwind.

"How can you be so sure, Zac?"

Zac smiled. "Call it a hunch," he replied.

3:45 rolled around, and the pool was a ghost town since the last fifteen minutes were reserved for adult swim. Which meant all the kids had either split or were gathering their belongings only to return the following day. All the lifeguards, except Alicia—who was sitting on Station 1 until 4 o'clock—were tearing down the umbrellas that canvased the tables when Ms. Cleveland's voice echoed out of the city pools intercom: "Zac Taylor, please come to the snack bar, you have a phone call." The request took Zac by surprise because nobody ever called him at work, everyone he knew would page him on his pager, and he would contact whoever it was when he was able, like all teenagers did.

He picked up the phone mounted to the left of the cooler, "Hello?" He waited, curious as to whose voice he'd hear on the other end. "Hey, baby, it's Mom," Janis said.

Zac's heart started to pound with anxiety. "Is everything alright?" he asked.

"Yes, dear, everything is fine. I just wanted to catch you before you left for the day. I'm making tacos, your favorite, tonight and wanted to let you know you're more than welcome to invite your friends. I'm making more than enough." Zac loved his mom's tacos, as did his crew, so he was defiantly down. "That sounds cool, Mom—what time were you thinking?"

Janis paused, probably checking a clock. "Well, it's almost 4 o'clock now, so how does about 6 o'clock sound?"

Zac figured two hours would give him plenty of time to smoke out with the boys before getting their grub on, "Yeah, sounds perfect. Is Rick going to be there, or his he working late again?" Zac crossed his fingers, hoping she would say he was working late.

"No, baby, he's already home. He took the afternoon off today. He wasn't feeling well," she replied.

Knowing Rick would inevitably fuck with his friends, Zac simply told his mom, "I'll ask my friends if they want to come, but you know how they feel about him being around. Either way, mom, I'll be there. I love you."

Janis replied, "I love you too, sweetheart. I'll see you when I get home from work."

As Zac hung-up the phone, he let out a deep sigh. Memories of his thirteenth birthday party flashed through his mind. He had blown out the candles on his cream-cheese frosted vanilla cake, and was fanning the smoking candles when Rick, who had been drinking all day, shouted, "Now that the boy's thirteen, maybe his balls will drop and he'll grow some hair like a man." The comment had embarrassed Zac immensely, as all of his friends were huddled around him cheering him on as he finished his birthday wish. The party went from ten kids laughing and cheering, to dead silence. Tears flooded his eyes, and he ran to his room, ending a birthday party he had been looking forward to all year. After that, Zac was always wary of hosting parties.

Zac returned to taking down umbrellas; however, he couldn't escape the fact that it was almost 4 o'clock and his mom still hadn't wished him happy birthday, and she hadn't mentioned anything about his birthday to frank. On the other hand, he was having tacos for dinner, not a bad consolation prize. Yet, he still couldn't fathom why she hadn't acknowledged his eighteenth birthday. To Zac, there were only five birthdays that actually mattered to people: thirteenth because kids become teenagers; sixteen, naturally, because one can obtain a driver's license; eighteen because one enters adulthood; twenty-one because of one's ability to purchase alcohol; and twenty-five because one's car insurance finally goes down substantially and he could finally rent a car if needed—so he had been told.

Zac walked over to Melany who was stacking lawn chairs near the toddler's pool, south of the Olympic sized pool that the older kids and adults utilized. As he approached, he said, "Hey, Mel, mom is making tacos—"

"Oh my God yes, I'm so hungry!" she yelled

Zac cracked up laughing, "Damn girl, you didn't even let me finish. What if I was going to tell you I can't hang out with you guys because I'm eating tacos with my parents," he stated.

Melany gave him her death stare.

"Okay, Okay, I was going to invite you," he quickly added, then helped her finish up stacking the chairs. "What about Jax, Mike, and Paul? Are they coming?" she asked.

Zac said he was about to page Double and Paul to find out if they wanted to come, explaining he'd ask Jax when he picked them up. While they waited for their boat ride, Zac took the opportunity to page Double and Paul using the phone in the snack bar. He waited about fifteen minutes, but neither of them called him back, which he found odd. He figured Paul would be difficult to get a hold of because he'd recently returned to Weatherford only three days ago after spending most of the summer visiting his grandparents in California. However, Double was finished at 3 o'clock and was usually quick to return a page, especially since he'd asked Zac to page him when they had concrete plans. Done with waiting alone by phone, Zac walked to the parking lot where Melany was sitting on the curb. "Did they call you back?" she asked.

"No, isn't that crazy—both of them know we're kicking it tonight, what's up with that?" Zac knew that if he couldn't get ahold of either of them, he'd have to sit and listen to his mom talk about how good of a couple he and Melany would make. He prayed, *please don't let Jax forget to pick us up, I need a wingman tonight!*

He was twenty-five minutes late, but Jax kept his word and picked both Melany and Zac up. "What up, bitches? Well, one bitch and a dude. Mel, I mean that with the utmost respect," Jax said as he stopped the boat a few feet from where they were sitting on the curb.

Melany let it slide because she felt horrible about Jax losing his job earlier.

Zac wasted zero time in asking, "What up, brother? So what do you think about eating my mom's tacos for dinner?"

Jax looked at him with wild eyes, "Do I have balls? Hell yeah, I want to eat your mom's taco!"

Melany snorted from laughing so hard.

Zac found little humor in it. Even so, he still gave his friend a high-five, for he knew that was some funny shit, he simply didn't want to acknowledge it.

"Hey, Z, is Rick going to be there?" Jax queried.

Regrettably, Zac had to inform him that Rick was indeed going to be there and told him he had taken a half day because he was sick or something. "You're still coming, right?" Zac probed. "Fuck yeah I'm still coming, Rick-the-Dick ain't keeping me away from your mom and her taco," Jax affirmed as he lost control with laughter. "I only wanted to know because if his ass is there, I'll be pulling up honking the shit out of old blue here." Jax tapped his steering wheel and continued, "You guys want to spark this joint I hocked from my old man's bureau?"

Zac raised his hand, offering Jax another high-five; he was on a roll adding, "Chris Chambers quote—well played, bro." (In Zac's eyes, no film, regardless of the genre, was superior to *Stand By Me.)*

"Hell yeah, my man—spark it up!"

Goose bumps rose on Zac's arm, for he believed that moment was magical, and it put a smile on his face, one that lasted quite a while.

They drove around town and smoked the joint that Jax had brought. After about 10 minutes, the joint was a roach, and neither of them were carrying roach clips, so Zac extinguished it by spitting in the palm of his left hand, instantly putting out the burning Zig-Zag. Before arriving at Zac's apartment for dinner, the three of them re-enacted the same routine from earlier that morning to remove any evidence of smoking.

Melany retrieved perfume out of her handbag, giving herself a couple of squirts. However, she didn't partake in smoking anymore with Jax and Zac. She knew Janis would ask her if she'd like to help out in the kitchen—something Janis did every time Melany had eaten with Zac and his family over the years.

Docking the boat as close to Zac's apartment as he could, Jax did what he told Melany and Zac he would. He laid into his horn saying, "Goddamn I love that shit! I think I can hear Dickie shouting from here." Both Zac and Melany chuckled. Not only because Jax actually honked the horn and held it down for about 30 seconds, but because of the devilish grin Jax wore while doing it; he genuinely took immense pleasure in pissing Rick off.

Melany was the first to depart the boat. "Alright, boys, I'm hungry, let's get a taco," she said before shutting her door. Jax and Zac looked at each other in astonishment, and Jax said, "I think she quoted Mr. White, dude." Last week they'd watched *Reservoir Dogs* for the hundredth time. There was no doubt she quoted the film, Zac agreed. Watching her walk toward the front door through the windshield of the boat, Zac whispered, "I love that girl, dude." Jax simply said, "I know, man,

I know." They both caught up with her and headed to the front door of Zac's apartment.

CHAPTER 7

WHO THE FUCK DID THAT?

Zac extended his right arm, reaching for the doorknob of his front door; however, before he was able to grab ahold of it, the door flew open to screams of, "Happy Birthday," hitting him as if he'd ran into a brick wall. He stood there bright eyed and frozen, completely confused as to what was happening. "What is all this?" he asked, realizing why Double and Paul hadn't returned his page. They were standing in the entryway of his apartment, along with Janis and Rick. Behind them, hanging on the hallway wall was a huge banner and balloons that read: Happy 18th Birthday!

Jax grabbed Zac's right shoulder, giving it a squeeze and said, "I told you this day would be epic, bro. Happy birthday, my man!" Then Jax made his way in to greet Double and Paul.

Janis instantly grabbed her son, giving him a huge hug while telling him, "Happy Birthday, Zachary!"

Zac hugged her back and whispered in her ear, "I was pissed at you all day, Mom—I thought you guys forgot."

She laughed adding, "Did you really think we'd forget *your 18th birthday*?"

Still curious about how his mom had pulled such a surprise off, he asked everyone, "How did you guys do all this?"

Jax explained to him that his mom had reached out to him yesterday asking if he could round everyone up to surprise him.

Zac was astonished. "All of you knew about this all day and didn't say anything!?"

Melany stepped in front of him making her way inside and said, "Wouldn't have been much of a surprise if we had, now would it?"

After greeting everyone, Zac thought to himself, *I've got the greatest friends in the world.*

Zac was following his friends into the living room when Janis quickly pulled him aside. She went on to explain to him that Rick had taken half the day off to set everything up, a gesture Zac would have never seen coming. "Really?" he asked. However, that wasn't the real reason she had pulled him aside adding, "He did, baby, I kind of fibbed about him not feeling well, but I wanted to warn you that after he setup, I came home to him watching that damn movie *Full Metal Jacket* again." Zac instantly understood. That was Rick's favorite film. He particularly enjoyed the basic training portion of the film, but then again, *who didn't?* Zac hugged his mom again and said, "Thanks for all this, Mom; it's pretty cool, and thanks for the heads-up as well. I'll be sure to thank him."

Janis took a step backward, looking up at her son while holding on to both of his shoulders, "I cannot believe my baby boy is eighteen. I wish your uncle could be here to see this," she said tearing up. Zac agreed, that would have been the icing on the cake.

Zac walked into the living room where all his friends were hanging out and pulled Paul out of his seat on the sofa near the fireplace. This was the first time he'd seen Paul since his return from California. Zac had first met Paul Colin in the second grade when Rick had moved the family to Weatherford. Zac only knew Melany at the time, but she always hung out with her girlfriends back then, leaving Zac to fend for himself. During his first recess that year, he noticed Paul playing tetherball by himself; probably because Paul was a bit different than the other kids. Paul was born with Amniotic Band Syndrome which affected his left hand. It was a condition that caused the fingers on that hand not to fully develop, and from what Zac remembers, was extremely painful. Because of the pain it caused him, his parents decided to have his left hand amputated, leaving Paul with what he referred to as his "nub."

Zac walked up to Paul that day because he didn't know anyone and he figured this kid might be looking for a friend as well. When Zac approached Paul to introduce himself, Paul's first words to him were, "Aren't you scared of this like everyone else?" as he held his left arm in the air. At first glance, it did take Zac by surprise, as it would any second-grader. However, Zac said the first thing that came to him, "Looks like we'll have to high-five right-handed." Paul smiled and they had been close friends ever since. Now as a young adult, Paul was the tallest of the crew: standing almost 6' 6". One wouldn't be able to tell from the way he dressed—grunge-like, but he was country as shit: the true definition of a redneck. His southern drawl was like none Zac had ever heard, but he was crazier than Jax and funny as hell. His family ran a cotton farm south of town. The farm itself was a few blocks from his actual house, making the large red barn that stood on their farmland an excellent place for him to throw parties, and he threw some crazy parties.

The two hugged each other tightly, both wearing smiles showcasing their joy of being reconnected after a couple of months of separation.

"How the fuck was Cali, man?" Zac asked.

Paul couldn't contain his smile. "Z, *Van Halen* knows what the hell they're talking about, those California girls got it going on!"

Zac stepped back and furrowed his brow with a sly smile, "You hooked up out there didn't you!?"

Paul held nothing back, as usual. "I didn't only hook up, Z, I nubbed the shit of this chick I met out there—several times, my friend. She loved this country nub," he declared.

When Paul said he "nubbed" a girl, it meant that he utilized his left arm in ways one would never imagine on a female. They had never actually met anyone he'd performed such actives with, but hearing his stories about it, with that southern drawl, was hysterical. Paul didn't play an instrument like the others but did possess a great love for music, especially alternative music. He did, however, perform with Jax during their junior year talent show. Even though he only played one maraca and sang backup vocals, he did a pretty damn good job, considering his voice.

"What part of Cali did you go to again?" Zac asked.

Paul said his grandparents lived in a town called Vacaville, somewhere near Sacramento. His grandfather was an Air Force Colonel and had retired at an Air Force base near there about fifteen years ago. It was a place he had spent almost every summer, and he loved going there. It was Paul's home-away-from-home. Paul was about to sit back down when Jax asked, "What the fuck is *Papa Roach*?" referring to the t-shirt he was wearing.

Paul looked down and stretched his t-shirt out, allowing all of them to clearly see the picture of a baby doll that appeared to be holding drumsticks the doll was using to bang on another baby doll. The name Papa Roach was written above it. "They're a local band out of Vacaville, and they might be my new favorite band."

Jax looked at Zac confused then blurted out, "Bullshit, you're a diehard Nine Inch Nails fan, and why the fuck would a band call themselves *Papa Roach*?" It was a fair question, seeing as everyone in the room, except Paul, concurred.

Paul told them that the girl he "nubbed" was tight with the guitar players little brother and she had taken him to see one of their shows. He said he even got to meet a couple of the members of the band and they were cool as shit. They had played a small venue, and the band was a cross between rock and hip-hop. Adding that out of all the concerts they had ever attended together, which was well over twenty, including his favorite, Nine Inch Nails, Papa Roach tore the stage up like a vodka spiked punch-bowl on prom night.

Double, who was sitting in Rick's pale-gray recliner—the only piece of furniture that matched absolutely nothing in the living room—asked, "So why do they call themselves *Papa Roach*?"

Paul wasn't positive, but said he heard someone at the show saying their name had something to do with roaches being the only thing to survive if the world went to shit, so he believed that to be the angle they were going for. "They'd be the last band standing." Then he concluded, "I'm telling you guys, they're gonna blow up, and you're gonna wish you had this mother-fucking t-shirt." Double looked up to the ceiling, shut his eyes and said, "I can respect that."

Zac and his crew continued to bullshit, getting Paul up to speed on everything they had done together over the last two months; even though all the juicy details rested in this morning's activities at the pool. Jax didn't share the details concerning his sexual encounter with Ms.

Cleveland, though. It wasn't because he didn't want to, he did. He didn't particularly care for Melany knowing what he had done, and he didn't think Double or Paul would be able to keep it to themselves. As the conversation died down, Zac asked, "So what time do you guys want to head to Luke's party?" His question fell on deaf ears it seemed, then Paul finally said, "Dude, Luke' party got squashed, bro. His parent's plans fell through, so no-go at his place. Not to worry, my number-one mother-fucker. As I was letting Double sample my California chronic on our way here, we bumped into my brother at Sonic. He said he'd reach out to Luke's brother and pick up the keg he purchased," adding that the festivities would be held out on his land.

Zac looked over at Double who was snoring in the La-Z-Boy and said, "That must be some good shit if it knocked his ass out."

No one could be more pleased than Melany that Luke's party was called off. As she was not a fan of Luke, or his older brother because they both hit on her, constantly. Looking pleased, she stood-up and said she was going to see if Janis needed any help in the kitchen preparing dinner. As she exited the living room Paul stood as well, "I'm gonna hit the pisser fellas, that Route 44 is screaming to exit my dick," he said laughing as he left the living room.

Paul was in the restroom for almost ten minutes before he returned. Upon entering, he told Zac and Jax that Double was out cold, "Man that chronic is no joke. I'm flying high." Zac and Jax laughed, and Jax asked, "Was it hard getting your zipper down in there with that one hand? Shit, Paul, I would have thought you'd have that shit down after eighteen years of experience." Jax must have forgotten how quick-witted Paul was because of his two-month absence.

"Nah, man, it was a pic of your sister that fell out of my pocket, so I thought of myself nubbing the shit out her while I rubbed one-off."

Out of nowhere, Double flew out of the La-Z-Boy, as if he'd been riding a mechanical bull and it hurled his ass from the saddle, laughing his ass off at Paul's cap on Jax.

Startled, Jax said, "What the fuck, Dub, you scared the shit out of me. I thought your ass was out cold." He placed his hands on his chest in an attempt to slow down his heart rate.

Double took a second to catch his breath from laughing so hard then asked, "What the hell was in that shit, Paul? I've never been this keyed."

Paul winked, "I told you, big-man, that's what they smoke out in Cali. Why the hell do you think I go every summer?" he added.

Double informed the boys he too had to take a leak and made his way to the bathroom.

Zac probed Paul, "So did you bring anything else back from Cali?"

Grinning, Paul leaned over and whispered, "I have a sheet of California Sunshine, boys!"

Jax gazed over at Zac—they were both wearing the same look, as in, *what the hell is California Sunshine?*

Paul continued. "It's only the best acid money can buy. I've been saving it for your birthday, bro." Acid was by far Zac's drug of choice. When Jax and Paul dropped, they did it for the mere fact of tripping balls, but Zac preferred to drop with Double. Because, like Zac, he, looked at dropping acid as a way of expanding his mind. The last time the two dropped together, they played chess for seven hours straight trying to discover a fool-proof plan on how to defeat the Chess Grandmaster, Bobby Fischer. Zac didn't drop acid often, but when he did, it had always been a great time.

Double returned to the leaving room holding his stomach and plopped back down in Rick's recliner.

Noticing Double's look of discomfort, Zac asked, "You alright, man?"

Double leaned back in his chair. "Yeah man, I got a mad case of the munchies right now. That shit Paul has is no joke, boys."

Zac told him to get back up, so they could go see if dinner was ready.

Double jumped out of the chair like he was the Flash, with Zac, Jax, and Paul following suit.

As they were about to head into the kitchen, Rick stomped into the living room, screaming with disgust, "Who did that!?" Rick paced in front of them, standing about five inches from their faces.

They all stood motionless in front of the sofa.

"Who the fuck—who's the slimy little communist, shit, twinkle toes, cock sucker over here that just signed his own death warrant by leaving pubic hairs on my clean toilet?"

Silence quickly fell between Zac and his crew.

"Nobody, huh? The fairy fucking Godmother did it!"

They were all freaking out as all four of them were high as hell—even more so for Double and Paul.

"Out fucking standing! I will PT you all until you fucking die! I will PT you until your assholes are sucking buttermilk! Was it you, you scroungy little fuck, huh?" he asked Jax as he stared at him nose to nose.

"Sir, no, sir!" Jax said shaking.

"You little piece of shit, you look like a fucking worm—I bet it was you!"

"Sir, no, sir!" Jax yelled again.

Out of nowhere and, completely unexpected, Double said, "Sir, I did it, sir!"

"Well, no shit," Rick said as he now stood nose to nose with Double.

"What do we have here, a fucking fat hairy man, Private Harry. I admire your honesty. Hell, you can stay here at my home and fuck my wife." Rick suddenly pushed Double down into the couch. Not hard, enough to get his attention—as if he didn't already have it. Rick had them all scared shitless, yet was still standing over Double. "You little scum bag! I got your name! I got your ass! You will not laugh! You will not cry! You will learn by the numbers I will teach you! Now get up on your feet!"

Double didn't hesitate. It was the fastest they had ever seen the big-man move. It looked as if he were about to cry. Meanwhile, Jax, Paul, and Zac had no clue about what the hell to do.

"You had best un-fuck yourself, or I will unscrew your head and shit down your neck!" Rick screamed as his voice increased with intensity.

"Private Harry, why did you come to my home?" Rick asked, demanding an answer.

"Sir, to eat sir!" Double replied.

"So you're an eater. Let me see your eating face!" Rick stated.

"Sir?" Double questioned.

"Your eating face: YYYYYUUUUUUMMMMM!" Rick screamed with his mouth wide open. "That's an eating face. Now let me see your eating face!"

"YUMMY!" Double shouted with his mouth open.

"Bullshit, you didn't convince me. Let me see your real eating face!" Rick continued.

"YYYYYYYYYUUUUUUUUUUUUUMMMMMMMM!" Double squealed. This time with his mouth stretched to its limits.

"You didn't scare me, work on it."

"Sir, yes, sir!" Double said with a hint of relief.

They thought Rick's fun had concluded, but then he jumped into Paul's face. "What's your excuse?" Rick questioned.

"Sir, excuse for what, sir?" Paul asked.

"I'm asking the fucking questions here, stubby. Do you understand?"

"Sir, yes, sir!"

"Well, thank you very much. Can I be in charge awhile?"

"Sir, yes, sir!" Paul yelled, praying Rick would leave him alone.

"Are you shook up? Are you nervous?" Rick inquired.

"Sir, I am, sir!"

Paul's eyes watered as he stood there quivering.

"Do I make you nervous?" Rick continued.

"Sir?" Paul asked.

"Sir, what? Were you about to call me an asshole?" Rick grilled.

"Sir, no, sir!" Paul replied.

"How tall are you, stubby?" Rick asked, looking up at Paul.

"Six-foot-six, sir!"

"Six-foot-six! I didn't know they stacked shit that high. You trying to squeeze an inch on me somewhere, Huh?"

"Sir, no, sir!" Paul declared.

"Bullshit! It looks to me that the best part of you ran down the crack of your momma's ass and ended up a brown stain on the mattress. I think you've been cheated!" Rick shouted.

"Rick!" What are you doing to those boys?" Janis questioned as she stepped around the corner, noticing all the boys standing at attention.

Rick shot her a grin and stated, "Oh nothing, baby, we were just messing around before dinner is all."

She didn't buy it, but didn't press the matter either. Informing all of them that supper was ready and instructed them all to wash-up.

Rick pointed toward the latrine, "You heard the woman, go wash up!" he demanded.

They all shuffled down the hallway single file, making their way toward the restroom.

As they moved along, Paul whispered, "What the fuck was that shit?" Adding that he had never been so scared in his entire life. Holding out his right hand he shared, "Look at how bad I'm shaking!"

Zac felt like a complete asshole. Informing all of them that he had forgotten to tell them that Rick had watched *Full Metal Jacket* that afternoon. They all knew Rick's favorite pastime was quoting movies, especially that one, however, never to such an extreme.

Jax was unable to refrain and yelled, "You forgot! How the fuck could you forget something of such importance! I shit my pants, man! No lie! There is shit in my pants, Z!"

Zac tried to apologize, but it didn't help. Even Double interjected, "Sorry ain't cutting this time, Z! Do you know how much therapy I'm gonna to need to get over this shit? I'm having my dad file a restraining order on that mother-fucker!"

All four boys stood crammed in the tiny restroom that possessed only one sink, taking turns to wash their hands, or in Paul's case, hand. When they were finished, they began to exit the bathroom, until Jax screamed at Double, "Dude, get those pubes off the toilet!" They all shared a brief laugh, which helped ease the tension.

Double removed the pubic hairs from the rim of the toilet and rewashed his hands.

Once he'd finished, they were able to compose themselves and headed to the kitchen for some well-deserved tacos. It was safe to say that regardless of where either of them pissed again, they all possessed a new found appreciation, leaving pubes behind was not an option.

CHAPTER 8

FREE BIRD

Zac and his entourage were making their way toward his front door excited to leave. Not only for the party Paul was hosting in Zac's honor but primarily to get the hell away from the drill sergeant. Zac was the last in line to step outside; however, he heard his mom's voice question from the hallway, "Zachary?" He turned as Melany, who was standing in front of him, whispered that they would be waiting outside for him. He faced his mom, "What's up, Mom?" he asked. Janis wished him happy birthday one last time because she'd be in bed by the time he returned later that night. Zac wrapped his arms around his mom, hugging her tightly and said, "Thanks again for dinner, Mom. You're the coolest!"

Janis, not wanting to release her grasp on her son, was pleased that she was able to make a part of his day special, adding, "Zachary, please be safe and don't stay out too late."

Zac leaned back and promised he would do both. He knew he still had to work in the morning and wasn't a big fan of dragging ass at work after a night of partying, especially in the hot Oklahoma sun.

It was slightly past 9 o'clock when Jax docked the boat next to Paul's red 1990 Chevy Silverado Step-side Pickup parked to the left of the barn. Pulling into the party, Zac was impressed by the massive crowd Paul had assembled in only a matter of hours—then again, word traveled fast in small Oklahoma towns. There were easily seventy to eighty kids scattered across an acre of flat farmland, all excited to party like it was 1999. Zac was immediately greeted by a crowd of screaming high school students that followed Paul's lead, "Happy Birthday, Z!" the crowd shouted, sending goosebumps up Zac's spine. Zac thought to himself, *Jax was right again,* this day was indeed turning into one he would never forget.

Jax, Melany, and Zac headed to greet Paul and Double who had left Zac's apartment together in Paul's ride. Paul was standing on top of a round hay bale that stood about seven feet high and about five feet in circumference. There were nearly forty of them lined-up in a row, easily covering fifty-yards in the distance. Double sat underneath where Paul was perched. Still appearing to be high from blazing before supper. After greeting Double in usual fashion, Double asked, "What up crackers?

Jax was the first to reply, "Glad basic-fucking-training is over."

Zac couldn't help himself, "You haven't forgotten about that yet? Fucking pussy!"

Melany, who had, fortunately, missed out on their "training session" snorted from laughing, as she noticed Jax becoming infuriated.

"Forget—fuck you, Z, I'm calling a shrink first thing tomorrow. That asshole messed me up."

The crew shared a laughed, and Paul added from above, "On the flipside, Z, pretty sure I caught your mom checking me out—I think she wants me to nub her!"

Zac had nothing, so he did what anyone would do in that predicament, and something Paul couldn't, he flipped him off, left-handed.

Paul jumped down from the hay bale and signaled for them to follow him into the barn so they could grab a beer. Following Paul's lead into the massive red barn they noticed, Byron, Paul's older brother, had put the tap on the keg and was opening a large plastic bag that contained 50-plus Red Solo Cups. "What up, Z! Happy birthday, man!" Byron said. Zac thanked him as Byron bestowed upon on him the first beer out of the keg, adding, "This Buds for you, my man." Zac held the cup up, a gesture of respect to the man that gave it to him. Once everyone had a beer in hand, Byron asked, "Z, you gonna play "Bucked-from-the-Bale?" Zac turned his attention toward the hay bales as he watched the first of many participants take their first few steps. Zac quickly said, "Not this night, man. Last time I did that shit my shoulder hurt for three weeks." The group shared a laugh at Zac 's expense, as they remembered that night well.

Bucked-from-the-Bale was a game Jax kind-of created out of a dare one night at one of Paul's previous parties. He was drunk as shit, and Paul thought it would be funny to see if he would get on the hay bales and take off running, so he dared him to do it. He made it about 10 steps before falling to the ground with a thud, luckily only spraining his left arm. To play the game it had to be dark enough outside that one could barely see their feet in front of them while they walked. The object of the game was to stand atop the seven-foot hay bales that stretched half the length of a football field. One person at a time would begin from the closest hay bale to the barn and run to the opposite end in a dead sprint. The victor would be he, or she, that made it the furthest without being "bucked" off the hay bales first. Seemed easy enough; however, throw in being drunk or high, and the game was probably the stupidest thing—safety wise—they had ever imagined into existence. Hell, even doing it sober was next to impossible. To that day, not one person had ever stopped safely at the end of the hay bales, and the game had sent a number of victims to the emergency room. To play, you have to either be crazy as hell or fucked up from partying too hard.

Last summer, Jax actually made it to the end of the hay bales; however, he couldn't see where the end was. So when he reached what was referred to as the finish line, he continued running like he was Forrest Gump. *He was running!* Everyone still thinks of him as somewhat of a God for making it that far, but Zac can only recall how he looked running with nothing underneath his feet. It's a story he can't tell without bringing tears to his eyes from laughing so hard. He might as well be describing Wile E. Coyote chasing The Road Runner, including the common visual of Wile E. running in the air after sprinting off a cliff before ultimately falling to the ground, unsuccessful in his quest to catch The Road Runner. No one can believe Jax still plays the game after breaking his right arm, two ribs on his right side, and getting seven staples on the crown of his skull that night. Even after enduring all that pain, he still plays every chance he gets.

Not wanting to miss a chance to showcase his skills, Jax pushed Zac to the side and backhanded Paul gently on the chest stating, "Let's go show these fuckers how this shit is done!" Paul slammed his beer like he was hitting a beer-bong, "Hell yeah, let's do this shit!" Paul said as the two of them ran toward the bales.

Melany looked over at Double and asked, "So what are you going to do, Mike?"

Double scanned the crowd then held his cup up slightly, "I'm going to finish this beer and find out where the black women are hanging out."

Melany looked at him perplexed and said, "Mike, you're the only black person in our school."

Double smiled at her and Zac as he walked toward the crowd, stretching out both of his arms, displaying his large wingspan, shouting, "What color do you think white girls are in the dark, Mel? Bring on the jungle-fever, Double's horny!" He disappeared into the crowd leaving Melany and Zac speechless and thinking that white girls would actually glow in the dark. The two of them stood there, not saying a word to one another, watching the party together. Melany was the first to break the somewhat awkward silence, "You want to go watch those fools kill themselves on the bales?"

Zac grabbed her hand, "I do," he replied.

She returned the gesture, and they walked hand-in-hand toward the bales.

Walking over to watch Jax and Paul, there was somewhat of a mosh pit developing as one kid had Metallica's song "Wherever I May Roam, "blaring out of the boom-box he had resting on the hood of his car. Another kid bumped into Melany as they passed by the pit, making some beer slosh out of her cup.

"Sorry, Mel, I didn't see you," the kid said before rejoining the other moshers.

Melany could see the mosher had pissed Zac off. Had the kid not apologized, Zac's reaction might have been a bit different. "Dumbass!" Zac stated as they continued on their way. He knew the kid didn't mean it, but Melany was his girl, or at least he dreamt she was.

Upon their arrival to the hay bales, they scanned the terrain; it was nothing but dirt. Zac didn't particularly want to sit in it, nor did he want

Melany too, so he ran over and retrieved the comforter Jax kept in his trunk for such occasions. "Nice thinking," Melany said as Zac spread it out, giving them more than enough room to sit back and enjoy the contest. They had the perfect spot; the nearly full moon was centered above the hay bales in the distance, providing enough light so they could make out the face of each contestant. The hay bale tournaments were, as usual, relentless, claiming victim after victim; kids literally fell off of them left and right.

Sitting there, so close to Melany and under the gorgeous moonlight, only one thought was running through Zac's mind, "God she looks beautiful."

She looked over at him, sensing he was staring at her, and asked, "What are you thinking about?"

Too scared to tell her the truth, he stated, "I really wish Uncle J would have been able to make it out here. I miss him, a lot."

Melany grabbed his left hand affectionately, adding, "He's here, Zac. Maybe not physically, but he's here."

Zac smiled. It wasn't a lie. He did really wish his uncle was there, but he desperately wanted her to know his feelings for her too.

After about 30 minutes, everyone's interest in the game appeared to decrease. Luckily, without anyone having to make an emergency room visit. Not having any luck with the ladies this night, Double noticed Melany and Zac lying down on the blanket chatting and decided to join them. "What up, ya'll, mind if I chill with you?" Double asked, slurring his words.

Melany moved to her right, pushing Zac over as she did so, "Of course you can," she said.

As the three of them sat there, Paul, who was now the only person standing on the hay bales, quickly grabbed everyone's attention by yelling, "Everyone, shut off the music and shut the fuck up!" To which everyone complied. You could hear a field mouse fart; it was *that* quite. With Jax now joining them on the comforter, they looked up at Paul as he addressed the crowd. Obviously now drunk, Paul continued, "I want to thank everyone for coming out tonight in honor of our boy Z's 18th Birthday!" The crowd shouted with delight as if they were at a concert and the lead singer was telling them to sing along. Paul proceeded, informing the crowd, "There's still a shit-load of beer in the keg, so quit sitting on your asses and drink the fuck up!" The crowd roared again.

Zac turned to Jax, "He's really fucked up, isn't he?"

Jax nodded in agreement as he searched for his cup.

They thought Paul's unprepared speech had concluded, but then he blurted out at the top of his lungs, "I can do anything!" His audience screamed and hollered, before coming to a brief silence.

Zac saw this as a perfect opportunity for his final remarks, putting both hands to his mouth he howled, "Oh yeah, clap!" An uneasy calm swept through the crowd, they couldn't believe what Zac had said.

Paul, still standing alone on the hay bales, held both of his arms in front of his face, looking at them with utter confusion. Realizing he couldn't clap due to having only one hand, he addressed the crowd a final time, "I can do *almost* anything!" The crowd roared with laughter, some so hard they threw-up. Jax and Double lost it as well, both quickly giving Zac a high-five. It was by far the best burn Zac had ever used on Paul—or anyone for that matter.

Melany also laughed; however, eventually, she leaned over and whispered into Zac's ear, "Someone watched *Buffy the Vampire Slayer.*"

Zac thought for sure no one would catch that one, hoping to claim the burn as his own. "Guilty," he said. "How is it you always bust me on shit like that?"

She rolled her eyes. "Zac, come on! You know that's one of my top-five movies, but well played," she said, smiling at him. They shared a laugh together then she asked, "Are you about ready? I should probably get home. It's almost midnight, and we both have to work in the morning."

Zac agreed. It had been a long day, and 6:00 a.m. would be there before he knew it.

Leaning over toward Jax, Zac asked, "You about ready to jet, brother?"

Jax said he was going to kick it at the party for a while longer, but told him to take the boat. He'd swing by the pool in the morning to retrieve it and handed Zac his keys.

Melany and Zac stood, then Double asked, "Where are you guys going?"

Zac told him they were going to bounce because they had to be at work early in the morning, as did Double, and offered him a ride as Paul sat down in Melany's place. Double, whose word slurring continued to worsen at that point, said, "Nah, Z, I'm sick. Well, not right now, but I will be in the morning."

Zac cracked up and told Paul and Jax to make sure Double got home safely. Zac thanked Paul for the party and apologized they didn't get the chance to try the California Sunshine he'd brought from California.

Paul replied, "You're more than welcome, Z, and we'll save it for another time, my friend."

With that, Zac and Melany made their way to the boat. As they did, Jax ran up to them from behind asking Zac, "Hey, Z, I forgot to ask, how was it?" Zac knew Jax was referring to how his birthday turned out, replying, "It was as you said it would be, bro. It was epic!"

Jax hugged his best friend and added, "Hell yeah it was! By the way, tell Army Ranger Rick to go fuck himself for me!"

Zac released Jax then walked Melany to the boat.

Zac walked around to the passenger side of the boat, retrieved the keys from his pocket, then unlocked and opened the door for Melany. Once she was inside, he shut the door and walked around the rear of the boat. When he looked through the rear window at her, he couldn't help but think of the movie *A Bronx Tale,* one of his top five films and "The Door Test." He could hear Sonny telling Calogero to dump any girl who doesn't reach over and unlock the door. Peering through the window Zac began to feel nervous, he loved her. He didn't want to dump her before he even got a chance to date her. Passing the window, he noticed she didn't reach over to lift the button like the girl in the movie. Depression replaced his nervousness as he reached for the door handle, hanging his head in sadness. About to insert the key to unlock the door, he heard the sound of the door unlocking, yet she didn't reach over. Melany did, however, hit the automatic unlock button on the passenger side instead. Zac beamed, looking into the sky before opening the door and thought, "Close enough for me!" He then took the captain's chair and sailed off.

The drive to Melany's house was only about fifteen minutes long, enough time for Zac to finally man-up and declare his love for the woman sitting to his right. He looked over at her thinking to himself, "This is your chance, tell her already," yet no words exited his mouth. He desperately tried to spit them out; however, all he could muster up was, "Today was a good day, wasn't it?" He sat there thinking, *Today was a good a good day? Who are you, Ice Cube? I'm fucking lame!*

She turned toward him and replied, "Yeah, it was. Even though I thought for sure, we were all going to jail when Ms. Cleveland asked if we were stoned."

They laughed, taking Zac's attention off his unintentional Ice Cube quote. Zac agreed; he thought they were going to get busted too.

Melany added, "You did a really good job throwing that *we took his car* bit in there. Lord knows I wasn't going to say a word."

Zac, trying to be funny once again, said, "Well, you know me, Mel. I do what I can do, the best I can do, when I can do it." He made her laugh again, making himself feel good as well.

They pulled into her driveway, and Zac shifted the boat into park.

"Well, Zac, I really did have a great time with you today. Will you please thank your mom for me again for having us all over for dinner? Her tacos are the best ever!" she said as she reached for the door handle.

Zac replied, "I will. Thank you for hanging out with me today and sorry we got you stoned at work."

She smiled and told him, "Don't be sorry, it was fun. I don't think I'll ever do it again, but it was fun." Melany opened the door and set one foot outside the car.

"Hey, Mel?" Zac questioned. He couldn't believe he held her up. He knew what he wanted to say, hell, he had rehearsed it in his mirror a million times, yet still nothing.

"Yeah," she replied in her tender voice, pulling her leg back into the car, she shut the door, staring at Zac with her beautiful blueish-green eyes.

Zac's heart was pounding, he was sure she could see the jugular vein in his neck pulsating.

"What is it, Zac?" she inquired, waiting for him to speak.

Zac opened his mouth, "I…"

Melany showcased her perfect smile, and asked, "You what?"

Out of nowhere, Zac felt as if his balls finally dropped and he was now a man, stating, "I like you!"

She gazed at him, seeming a bit confused, "I like you too, Zac."

"No," he said, " I *like* you like you."

Melany looked a bit stunned, definitely speechless.

Her silence was unnerving, and Zac couldn't close the floodgates now. He started rambling, and even though he could hear himself telling himself to shut-up, he couldn't this time. He needed her to know how he felt, and he was in too deep now, there was no turning back at this point. Time to plead his case. He went on a long rant, informing her that he liked her liked her, as in, he wanted to be with her liked her. He explained how he's liked her since he realized how amazing she was way back at the heritage festival held over the Fourth of July weekend the summer after their fifth-grade year. Zac went on about how he had wanted to tell her how he felt for so long but was afraid he would ruin their friendship. Not only that but perhaps lose her as a friend entirely. Zac added the fact that he wasn't telling her because he wanted her to feel the same, which was utter bullshit, that's precisely what he wanted, but he didn't want her to feel pressured to feel the same because he'd finally confessed how he felt.

She held up her hand, stopping his rant mid-sentence, looked him directly in his eyes, leaned over the console, placed her hands on each side of his face, and said, "You talk too much," then leaned in and kissed him.

His eyes were still open as she kissed his lips for the first of what would eventually be many times, Zac thought, *Holy shit, we're kissing. Kissing with tongue!* A calm suddenly came over him as he tried desperately to focus on his kissing technique. As he became more comfortable with his performance, he felt an unexcepted stiffness possess his manhood. He was now sporting what he believed to be the biggest boner he had ever erected. Suddenly, he went from trying to focus on this magical moment he'd dreamt of for years, to thinking, *How the fuck am I going to hide this from her!?*

Melany's lips left Zac's, and she opened her eyes, noticing his eyes now closed, still performing his kissing maneuvers, which again made her laugh. A few seconds passed before Zac finally came too, and realized she was laughing at him. He opened his eyes, looked at her, and all he could do was smile.

Melany sat there and confessed to Zac that she had liked him for a very long time as well. Zac sat in disbelief, asking, "Why didn't you say anything?" Melany shrugged her shoulders. "I suppose for the same reasons you didn't. I cherish our friendship, Zac. You mean more to me than anyone, and always have." Melany leaned over, kissing him tenderly once again before opening her door and exiting the boat. Before she shut the door, she said, "Happy birthday, Zac."

Zac smiled and replied, "Thank you, Mel."

About to turn the key to begin his drive home, Zac stopped, and thought, *Wait a second!* He exited the vehicle, sprinting to catch Melany before she reached her front door. When he caught her, he tapped her left shoulder, then immediately bent over; huffing and puffing, desperately trying to fill his high and air-depleted lungs.

"Yeah?" she inquired.

Zac stood erect. "Does this mean we're a couple now? Like boyfriend and girlfriend?"

She grinned and asked, "Is that you want?"

Zac barely allowed her to finish her question, "Hell yes!" He coughed, and tried to be cool, "I mean, sure, if you're cool with it."

She pulled him close to her and went in for another kiss.

Zac and his boner quickly became reacquainted as he tried frantically not to stab her in her bellybutton with it as her body pushed against his.

Her lips left his once again, and she said, "That's exactly what I want us to be, Zachary Taylor." She turned and opened her front door; however, before walking inside, she said, "I'll see you tomorrow. Happy birthday again, Zac."

Zac stood there amazed. "Happy birthday. Fuck, I mean, yes, and thank you," he said, laughing at himself.

She laughed, walked inside, and shut the door behind her.

Zac took a minute to soak in what had transpired, standing there staring at the front door of his girlfriend's house. Strolling back to the boat he thought, "I'm going out with Melany Summers! Melany Summers is *my girlfriend!*"

Zac hopped back into the boat, lit a dagwood he recovered from the glovebox, started the engine, and began flipping through pages of Jax's CD folder, searching for the one song that could help express his current state of mind. Feeling as if the shackles from the seven-year-friend-zone sentence were finally removed, Zac felt like he had been paroled, and was now free as a bird. He found Lynyrd Skynyrd's CD about five pages in, inserted it, and sailed home. He didn't think his life could get any better—he too felt fine!

CHAPTER 9

WINNIE

Allen Collins fantastic guitar solo in "Freebird" had concluded when Zac turned onto Bond Street, where he lived. In the darkened distance, he noticed what appeared to be a large bus parked alongside the curb in front of his apartment complex. *What the fuck is a bus doing around here?* he wondered. A reasonable question, seeing he couldn't recall ever seeing anything like it parked around his neighborhood in the 10-plus years he had lived there. As he approached the vehicle, he realized what he thought was a bus, was actually a white Winnebago mobile home with yellow trim. He parked the boat directly behind the Winnebago, as the mobile home was in front of his family's apartment. The boat's headlights lit up the rear of the Winnebago, and Zac took notice of the personalized license plate that hung below the spare tire, which was covered by a custom-made tire cover with a large, yellow, Grateful Dead dancing bear. The license plate was also familiar, registered in California and personalized with the slogan: GD#1FAN.

A burst of excitement rushed through Zac's body as he exited the boat as fast as he could. So quickly that he tried to depart before removing his seatbelt: a maneuver that flung him back into the captain's chair without mercy. *What the fuck?* Zac thought, unable to escape his confinement fast enough, desperately attempting to push the release button of the seatbelt buckle. Now standing in front of the boat, he gazed up at the massive motorhome that sat parked in front of him. He observed the curtained rear window, noticing there were dancing bear stickers, each one a different color, all along the bottom of the window. Zac knew those stickers well as they were the merchandise of his Uncle J's favorite band, The Grateful Dead.

Zac walked to the side of the Winnebago closest to the curb, in an attempt to find the door, as he had zero doubt this was indeed his uncle's recreational vehicle. Zac ran his hand along the side of the Winnebago as he walked, marveling at its beauty and enormity. While trying to see into any window that might share confirmation of who was inside, Zac's curiosity was quickly replaced with agony as he tore a chunk of skin off his left shin by walking directly into the metal stairs that led to the main entrance of the mobile home. Falling into his yard, yelling obscenities loud enough to wake everyone in the neighborhood, he vigorously tried to rub the pain away. Loud stomps emerged, coming from the rear of the Winnebago, scurrying to the front. The main light of the mobile home now illuminated most of the vehicle, and Zac saw a massive shadow behind the curtain that canvased the front door as it quickly opened.

A long-haired, bearded man peered out, scanning the yard, searching for the source that had violently shook his home on wheels. Instantly, the man took notice of a younger man lying in the grass holding his leg in discomfort—the young man he had traversed the country to see on this extraordinary day.

Zac recognized the man who was looking down at him, a man that was now laughing hysterically at his expense. Uncle Jimmy stood in the open doorway of the Winnebago wearing a tie-dyed Grateful Dead t-shirt, board shorts, and a pair of Birkenstock sandals: his usual attire.

Stepping down from the metal stairs that Zac had recently become intimately acquainted with, Jimmy stood, welcoming Zac with open arms. Zac returned to his feet, jumped into his uncle's warm embrace, and asked, "What are you doing here? I thought you were working?"

Jimmy hugged his nephew tightly, "You didn't really think I'd miss your 18th birthday did you?" he said.

Zac was still in shock, unable to believe how great his birthday had actually turned out to be.

Bugs began to enter the open door of the Winnebago, all flying toward the fluorescent light fixture on the midnight blue roof. "Shit, bugs are getting in. Come on, I'll give you the dime tour," Jimmy said as both of them began to swat the bugs back outside.

Zac took one step into the mobile home, and his jaw dropped in astonishment as this was no normal Winnebago.

"This, my son, is Winnie," Jimmy said, holding out his arms like he was Vanna White displaying merchandise some contestant had won.

Zac's captivated eyes scanned the entire interior, from his left to his right, he couldn't believe all of the custom work his uncle had put into Winnie. She came equipped with two captain's chairs up front, a stand-alone captain's chair to the immediate right, and a sofa that sat across from the stand-alone chair. There were two cushioned bench seats resting under the kitchen table to his immediate left; all of which displayed custom tie-dyed upholstery, each including an embroidered dancing bear in a different color. Zac had never seen anything like it. It was as if he were looking at a canvas splashed with various paints and trying to find the hidden images among a kaleidoscope of colors. It was evident his uncle had spared no expense.

On the center of the kitchen table, there was a giant decal of the famous red and blue Grateful Dead skull with a lightning bolt in the center. It was the largest image of the skull Zac had ever seen, and having an uncle that sold thousands of them, he'd defiantly seen his share. Winnie was also equipped with a TV and VCR above the stand-alone captain's chair, a nice sized refrigerator, freezer, stove, microwave, shower, bathroom, and every other amenity one might desire—all of which was customized and on theme. Even the knobs of each cabinet featured embossed images of the dancing bear heads.

Jimmy walked to the rear of Winnie and said, "Zachary, follow me."

Zac obeyed, limping as he followed.

Uncle Jimmy pulled a large Grateful Dead curtain to his left, unveiling the master bedroom. "This is my sex den, son," Jimmy stated.

Zac looked at the large bed in the middle of the room that appeared to be at least a Queen-size. "Your bed is a fucking circle, man!" Zac exclaimed.

Jimmy laughed, while resting his arms on his belly, "You bet your ass. It's the latest California dream," he replied.

Zac scanned the rest of the room: to his right there was another TV and VCR with a Super Nintendo hooked-up to it as well. There were cabinets above the bed, along with nightstands on either side of it, all featuring the same customization as the furniture up front. Winnie indeed was a work of art.

Zac's tour of his uncle's castle on wheels concluded as he heard his uncle call from behind, "Come on up front, I got something for you."

Zac took a seat at the table, tracing the large skull decal on top of it with his right finger. Zac's curiosity had gotten the best of him, "How much did this thing cost you?" he asked as his uncle was retrieving something from the cupboard above the stove.

"You know, you're in good company sitting at that table. Jerry himself shared a few meals with me, sitting in that very spot," he said, obviously trying to avoid the question. Jimmy retrieved a thin, long shaped package and handed it to Zac.

"What's this?" he asked, inspecting the gift wrapped in tie-dye wrapping paper.

His uncle smiled. "Just open the damn thing!"

Zac tore the package open like he was a five-year-old on Christmas day, excited as hell to reveal the contents. Zac's anticipation halted as he read the words on the present: "Map of the United States." Confused, he looked up at his uncle, "A map?"

Jimmy laughed, adding, "I swear, your generation is fucking obtuse! What are they teaching you kids in public schools these days?"

Unfold the damn thing, son."

Zac again complied to his uncles' demands, unfolding the map five times before it displayed all the states and highways of North America. Zac scanned the map and noticed nothing out of the norm. "Well?" Zac questioned.

Jimmy looked down at him disappointed, "For fuck'sake, son!" he shouted as he pointed to the middle of the map. Upon further investigation, Zac noticed that Kanas City had a small, blue-inked, circle around it. "Why is Kanas City circled?" he asked, still baffled at what his uncle was getting at.

Jimmy took a seat at the table, opposite of Zac, "I'm heading there on the 9th, and I want you to come with me. What do you say?"

Zac's eyes returned to the map, butterflies began dancing inside him, "I'll have to quit work early, but hell yes I'll go with you!" he exclaimed.

Jimmy reached across the table, and squeezed his nephew's right shoulder. "Well happy fucking birth, boy!"

As the two sat, Zac quickly did the math in his head, "Wait, that's two days from now. Rick will never let me quit work early and go with you."

Jimmy sneered, smoothly stroking his long, gray-haired beard, and calmly said, "You let me handle ol' Rickey. You grab the chessboard out of the cabinet I pulled your gift from. You have yourself an ass-whooping coming."

Zac stood to retrieve the board. "Good luck, old man, I got something for you," he said, noticing his uncle was pulling a dugout one-hitter from his shorts pocket. "Oh, it's on, young-buck," Jimmy retorted.

Zac laid the board out on the table and began setting it up while Jimmy lit the one-hitter and played with the portable CD player resting on the table, "You like the Grateful Dead?" Jimmy asked rhetorically, trying to hold in his hit simultaneously.

Zac chuckled as he discreetly placed a white pawn in his right hand and a black pawn in his left hand, then put both arms behind his back, hiding the pieces from his uncle so he could choose one and decide who'd get the first move.

"Left," Jimmy hollered.

"Fuck me! I hate being white," Zac declared.

Both Zac and Jimmy preferred to be black, as they were both defensive chess players. According to their rules, white always went first, meaning Zac would be on the offense; however, he still made the best of it.

The two played for over forty-five minutes, swapping stories to catch up. Jimmy told Zac about his cross-country travels and repeated stories that Zac had heard a 100 times. But Zac didn't mind; Jimmy was a fascinating storyteller and always told the most amazing stories. Zac, in turn, shared all the events that transpired on his unbelievable 18th birthday, beginning with Jax's ping-pong story, all the way up to his balls dropping, and him asking out the woman of his dreams. It was the perfect end to an epic day.

CHAPTER 10

THE DAY THE MUSIC DIED

Zac woke in his bedroom to the jarring sound of Janis' voice echoing from the dining room, "Jimmy!" Zac leapt out of bed and sprinted toward her. He turned the corning off the hallway, entered the room, and saw his uncle lying on the floor holding his chest, gasping for air. He looked like an actor about to pass away; this couldn't be real. Zac's training instantly kicked in. He scanned the room, his mom was standing frozen next to the kitchen table, with her chair flipped on its back behind her. Rick was standing over Jimmy, only a foot or two away. Zac instructed his mom to call 911 then shouted, "What the hell happened?"

Rick stood dumbfounded, "We were talking, and..." he didn't have the words.

Zac knelt at his uncle's left side on the cold kitchen floor. He didn't have time to think, only act. His right ear hovered over Jimmy's mouth as he listened for breathing while looking to see if his chest was rising. His breathing and pulse were faint but present. There was no need to perform CPR, he could only comfort his uncle as they waited for the paramedics to arrive. "Don't you die on me!" Zac yelled.

Jimmy pulled Zac close to him, struggling to get his words out.

"What is it, Uncle J?" Zac asked as tears seeped out of his eyes and ran down his flushed cheeks. Zac held Jimmy's head in his arms.

"It's Jerry's…" Jimmy said as the air exited his body. His eyes went dark as they stared blankly at the ceiling.

"It's Jerry's what?" Zac anxiously questioned. The paramedics rushed through the front door, set their medical bags down beside Jimmy, and pushed Zac out of the way.

After 20-minutes of compressions, Jimmy still had no pulse. Jimmy was gone.

The paramedic that had pushed Zac out of his way reached to his right shoulder, pressed the button on his black radio, "We have a DOA, bring in the stretcher and bag," he said.

Zac was confused, "What do you mean DOA? Help him!" he demanded.

The paramedics shook his head. "Son, we tried, there's nothing we can do at this point. I'm sorry, he's gone," he replied.

Zac refused to accept it. "Shock him—do something!" Zac demanded.

Janis reached out for Zac, hoping to provide him some sort of comfort, not only for him but for herself as well.

Zac pushed her away, "What did you guys do to him?"

Janis and Rick said nothing.

A third paramedic walked into the apartment with his back toward everyone, pulling a stretcher that had a black-leather body bag resting on top of it, followed by two police officers.

Zac fell to the floor as they began to put Jimmy into the bag. He felt as if he were in a dream. Only a few hours ago, he and Jimmy were playing chess and catching up. This had to be a nightmare.

Two of the three paramedics lifted the bag on each end, gently placing Jimmy's lifeless body on the stretcher. "We will be taking him to Memorial Hospital. Ma'am, are you the next of kin?" the third paramedic asked Janis.

She could barely breath, but somehow found a way to answer, "I am. He never married."

The paramedic informed her that there would be some paperwork for her to sign. "There's no rush, but they will need you to come by within the next 72 hours," he added.

Janis again reached out for her son.

"Get off of me! You guys are dead to me!" Zac shouted as he pushed her off of him and ran outside toward Winnie.

Janis yelled, "Zachary!"

Rick grabbed Janis by the arm as she lunged toward Zac. "Let him go, give him space," he said.

She quickly spun around, and slapped Rick on his right cheek, "You did this! Had you agreed to let Zachary go, he'd still be here!" Janis stated as she snatched her purse off the table and followed the paramedics out of the apartment.

CHAPTER 11

IT'S JERRY'S...

Melany looked down at her silver-and-gold-linked watch: it was almost eight-o-clock and still no sign of Zac. She thought to herself, *he's never late on Monday, I need to page him,* as she walked as fast as her legs would move her to the snack bar. She retrieved the handset and pushed the buttons on the dialer, number by number, sending 911 to his pager, praying nothing was wrong with her new boyfriend.

Twenty minutes passed as Melany continued to monitor her watch. She exited the snack bar, slamming the door behind her, and scanned the parking lot for Jax's boat through the chain-linked fence. There was no sign of the boat; however, in the distance she spotted Jax's dad's '76 Monte Carlo turning right into the parking lot. As Jax approached, she noticed Double sitting shotgun. Melany's heart dropped. *What the hell is going on!* she thought.

Double rolled down the dirty, mud-canvased window, "What up girl?" he greeted in his normal morning tone. She was beginning to panic, "Why isn't Zac with you?" she questioned.

"What you talking about, Willis? Isn't he here with you?" Double replied.

"No!" is all she could spit out.

Jax shouted, "Get the fuck in!"

As the three of them approached Bond Street, they took notice of a red and gold ambulance turning left on to Sherman Street with its lights off. They inched closer.

"Is that Z's mom?" Jax said, pointing at Janis's orange, rusty '88 VW Rabbit, following close behind the emergency vehicle.

Melany pushed the trash on the rear passenger seat to the floor. Bracing herself, she rose in her seat, stretching the seatbelt to limit. "That's her!"

Janis passed without noticing them, following half a car link behind the ambulance.

Their eyes stared, fixated on Janis. "No one's with her!" Melany shouted. Holding her hands to her mouth in panic, tears began to roll down her porcelain face.

Jax turned his head to his to his right, gripping the steering wheel with all his might. "I'm flipping this bitch around!" he informed them.

Double turned toward Jax. "Nah, dude, go to Z's crib! It's right around the corner. We can go to the hospital after," he demanded.

Jax adjusted, slamming the breaks. His front tire hit the curb in the opposite lane, barely making Bond Street.

Approaching Zac's apartment, they noticed Rick turning to head inside. He reached for the front door as he heard tires grinding on the asphalt behind him. The smell of melting rubber replaced the crisp summer morning as the car came to an abrupt stop, leaving embedded tire marks behind.

Melany flew out of the vehicle, mortally terrified. "Where is he!?" she screamed.

Startled, Rick turned toward the commotion, "Melany?" he questioned with squinted eyes.

Jax and Double ran behind her toward Rick.

"Where's Zachary?" she asked.

Rick pointed out into the yard toward Winnie behind the apartment complex. "He's in that," he said.

They turned and noticed Zac peering from the curtain in the far left window of the recreational vehicle. They all stood baffled, trying to make sense of everything.

Jax was the first to speak, "What the fuck is that?" he asked.

Rick stepped into the apartment, "It's Jimmy's," he replied, before shutting the door behind him.

Winnie's doorknob turned, opening the main cabin door. Zac stood sobbing in the doorway.

It took mere seconds for Melany to jump into his arms, "What is it, baby," she said.

Zac absorbed her into his arms; it was the closest thing to comfort he had felt all morning.

Jax and Double stood on the curb, looking into Winnie, trying to figure out what the hell was going on.

Double turned his attention to Zac. "Z, what's going on, man?"

Zac backed up, releasing Melany, and took a seat of the sofa. His throat was dry as he searched for the right words. He couldn't look them in the eye. His head sank in sorrow. "Uncle J…he's…" Zac struggled.

Jax stepped inside Winnie, taking the closest seat next to his best friend, and did his best to comfort Zac. "Take your time, man. Uncle J's what, Z?" he asked.

Zac slowly raised his head, his face red. "Uncle J's…dead!" he said weeping.

Jax gripped him tightly, as did Melany and Double. Neither of them had the words, there were no words. Uncle Jimmy was Zachary's everything, and the three of them knew this more than anyone else. His friends did the only thing they could do, they held him; held him in painful silence for what seemed forever.

Double hesitantly probed with uncontrollable curiosity, "Z, what happened, bro?"

Zac's lips quivered. "I was lying there in my bed man, about to get up. I heard my mom scream. I ran. I ran as fast as I could. When I got to the kitchen, he was lying on the floor. I couldn't do anything! I should have done something!" Zac broke down again. He couldn't control his emotions, he felt broken.

Double put his arm back around his friend. "We got you, man—we got you."

Melany gently stroked Zac's back, doing her best to provide him any sort of solace. "Did he say anything? Anything at all?" she asked.

Zac grabbed the bottom of his white t-shirt, and wiped his eyes and nose. "He said, "It's Jerry's…" then he was gone."

Everyone looked confused.

"What do you think, "It's Jerry's" means?" Jax questioned.

Zac stared down at the carpeted the floor. "I have no clue."

Melany looked over Zac's back toward Jax and Double and silently mouthed, "What do we do?"

The two looked back at her. Double was on the other side of Jax, furthest away from Zac, and threw up his arms to indicate they didn't know.

An hour passed as the four of them sat in mourning. Each one of them had many fond memories regarding Uncle Jimmy, for they had spent many evenings with him during past visits. This wasn't only Zac's loss, it was their loss. Uncle Jimmy was the reason each of them stuck with band, he taught them everything he knew about loving and respecting music as an art form, and it all started with The Grateful Dead.

Zac stood abruptly, turned around, and faced his friends. "Okay, it has to mean something," he said, wiping his swollen, tear-soaked face with his arm.

They looked up at him, "What are you saying, Z?" Double questioned.

Zac told them how Uncle Jimmy was in Winnie when he returned home late last night. Explaining that they had spent a few hours catching up, and how Uncle Jimmy had given him a map of the U.S. as he retrieved it from the kitchen table. "Look, Kanas City is circled. We were going to leave tomorrow to go there," he said, pointing almost directly to the middle of the map.

The three of them followed his finger. "Wait a second—who's Winnie?" Jax interrupted.

Zac stared at his best friend. "That's what you got from all that?"

Double and Melany laughed, which put a brief smile on Zac's face.

The three of them stood, almost in unison. "Do you think it's regarding something in Winnie?" Melany asked.

Zac told them he didn't know, but he knew there was one way to find out. He rotated toward the sex den. "Let's start looking back there," he said. He pulled back the tie-dyed curtain that served as a door.

"What the fuck! He has a round bed?" Jax asked as he stepped into the room.

Zac nodded. "Evidently, it's the latest California dream." He instructed Double and Jax to search the closet. He took the left side of the room, while Melany rummaged through the right.

"Z, you might want to check this out," Jax said from the closet.

Zac and Melany stopped their search, "What is it?" Zac asked as he stood behind Double's massive frame. Both of them pointed toward the floor. Resting underneath Uncle Jimmy's hung wardrobe was a personal safe. A safe that stood about three feet tall and three feet wide.

The lock resembled their school lockers, but this one was a bit larger, and the numbers went up to fifty.

Zac pushed his friends gently to the side and knelt down, shoving the hanging clothes out of the way.

"Do you know the combination?" Melany asked.

"No. He didn't show me this," Zac said. He tried to think..."It's Jerry's...It's Jerry's—*what* Uncle J?" An eternity passed, thoughts of past conversations with his uncle flooded his mind, like a tsunami drowning a city.

"Do you think it's Jerry's birthday?" Double asked.

Zac dropped to his knees as he patted his large friend on the back, signaling a job well done. A memory of Zac and his uncle quickly came to mind: he was about to be twelve. The two were eating dipped-cones to celebrate Zac's birthday prematurely. They were sitting outside at a picnic table in a park near a bronze statue of some local war hero. "Zachary, on this day, way back in 1942, my hero was born. Do you know who that is?"

"I do, Uncle J; it's Jerry Garcia, right?"

"That's correct, son. Jerry and his band, The Grateful Dead, put me on the journey I'm on today. A journey of helping people find their path, or purpose in this world.

Zac cleared the dial.

"Zachary, there is really only one bit of advice I can give you…"

He turned the dial to the right: 08. The memory continued, he could hear J's voice, "Know where you're going, son…" Two rotations to the left: 01. "And, know what you're going to do when you get there. You do that, and there is nothing you can't accomplish." Back to the right: 42. Back to the left…Click.

CHAPTER 12

WHO'S TINY?

Jax, Double, and Melany leaned over Zac's left shoulder, trying to sneak a peek at the contents of Uncle Jimmy's safe. The metal hinges of the door creaked like something out of a horror film as Zac opened it slowly. Thin beams of sunlight from the closet window provided little assistance in feeding their curiosity. If they were going to see anything, Zac would have to pull whatever rested inside, out, into the light. As he did, their eyes widened with every item retrieved.

"Is that?!" Jax belched, seeing a brick-sized package wrapped in cellophane.

"Holy shit!" Double said as Zac handed him the compressed marijuana. Double added, "Dude, this is like five pounds!"

Zac smiled at his friends and said, "Guess we won't need any bud for a while!"

Zac's attention returned to the safe. Next to where the brick of bud had resided, he recovered a black, tin box. Taking notice of its weight, he placed it beside him on the light-blue carpet. "This thing is fucking heavy!" he said.

Jax stooped, hoping to get a closer look.

Melany and Double leaned over as Zac released the silver hinge that secured the lid.

"Shut up!" Melany shouted.

Inside was two stacks of $100 bills, each wrapped tightly with an orange paper band that read: "ten-thousand dollars." Zac reached his left hand over his shoulder, handing one of the stacks to Jax, who thumbed the freshly-printed currency. Neither of them had ever seen anything like it, and there was another one where that came from.

Zac kept his focus on the safe, continuing to extract items one-by-one. The next was an official document from the state of California. It's solid blue border demanded notice and read: "State of California," in bold white lettering. He held it up. "This is the title to Winnie," he said, passing it to his friends.

Double was the first to read the document, affirming, "Z, he owns this thing?"

Zac turned to Double, "I know, man. He told me it was his pride and joy." His search resumed, as he discovered another official document from the state, that read: "California Last Will and Testament." His heart sank, tears began to flow as he scanned the text: 1st Beneficiary: Zachary Isaac Taylor.

Melany gently pushed Jax to the side, taking his place next to Zac after realizing what the document was, doing her best to comfort her new boyfriend and old friend. "It's okay to cry, baby, it's okay."

Jax looked at Double like a dog trying to decipher an odd sound.

Double shot back a, *what the fuck are you looking at me for*, look.

Jax didn't hold back, "What the hell is going on?" he questioned, diluting the solace of the moment.

"What are you talking about, dude?" Zac asked, wiping tears from his eyes.

"That's the fucking second time I've heard Mel call you baby! What the shit!?"

Jax always had a way of making odd situations extremely awkward.

Melany looked at Zac. *Can I tell them?* her eyes questioned.

Zac signaled, yes.

"He asked me out last night. Finally!"

Double and Jax dogpiled the two, embarrassing them both.

Zac's tears were replaced with intervals of laughter and pain. "Dude, you're fucking crushing me!" he exclaimed, pushing his way out of confinement.

Double thrusted himself up, and noticed something in the back of the safe, "Yo, Z—what's that?"

Zac reached his arm into the back of the safe. Double was right, there was something there. It was a black Rolodex.

The Rolodex was jam-packed with white index cards. Unlike the one his mother owned, this one was almost entirely full of contacts. Zac flipped through each card, one-by-one as fast as he could.

"What are you doing?" Jax asked.

Zac held up his finger, demanding a moment of quiet while he rummaged through cards. Flipping one after another, as fast as his hands would allow, he briefly paused at the "T's," holding the contact in place with his left index finger while searching the remaining cards with his right.

Zac stood, still holding one card in place, "Come with me," he demanded as the three of them followed suit.

Walking into the galley, Jax wouldn't shut up, "I so see you guys being that couple that gets married after graduation and stays married for like

50 years. Then one of you will die around 70 and the other will be stuck trying to figure out how to have sex with another person because you've only been with each other. That shits gonna be hilarious."

Double put his hand over Jax mouth, "Dude! Too far!"

Zac took a seat at the kitchen table, pointed to the map next to Jax, on the opposite side of the table. "Jax, hand me that!" he demanded.

Melany and Double gazed at each other confused, both trying to figure out where Zac was going with this. As Jax handed him the map, Zac informed them that Uncle J had gifted him the map last night as a birthday gift, further explaining his intentions to take Zac to Kanas City on the 9th.

After unclasping the index card from the Rolodex, Zac placed it gently on the displayed 50 states, just above Missouri.

Melany grabbed the card to investigate it further, "Who's Tiny?" she asked.

Zac shrugged, adding, "Uncle J never mentioned them before, but this is the only card in here that has a Kanas City address, and that's where he was taking me," he said, pointing to the circled city on the map.

"What are you saying, Z?" Jax questioned.

Zac paused and let out a shallow sigh, then glanced at Melany and over to Double and Jax. "You guys down for a road trip?"

Jax and Double smiled as if they were stepping into a strip club for the first time.

"I am not going to be the only girl!" Melany protested.

Zac knew who she was going to ask to ride along, adding, "So that's a yes?"

Excited, Jax and Double simultaneously shouted, "Hell yeah!"

CHAPTER 13

GOING TO KANSAS CITY

Four hours had passed since Zac's friends departed to collect their bags for the trip. He stared upward, focusing on the air vent directly above his head as the melancholy melodies of "Lightning Crashes" by Live resonated in his eardrums. The familiar sound of automobile brakes coming to a halt interrupted his mindless confusion. Thinking to himself, *Please don't be here for me,* he sat up and hurried to the other side of the bed. Looking out of the curtain, he saw his mom stepping out of her vehicle. Her face beet red, cheeks swollen, tainting her usually flawless complexion; no doubt she was crying from her devastating loss. Zac followed her footsteps with his ears, hoping they led her into the apartment and not Winnie's front door.

Knock! Knock! "Zachary, are you in there, honey?" Her voice was raspy.

Standing there, she realized she wasn't actually prepared to speak with her son—perhaps her motherly instinct had guided her; Still, Janis knew she needed to set the record straight with him. "Please open the door, Zachary! I can feel your movement from out here."

Zac looked down at his feet resting on the floor at the foot of the bed, *Shit!* he thought, *I didn't think about that.*

A strong gust of wind felt as if it could carry her off to the land of Oz. Her long hair whipped violently against her cheeks. She placed her left hand on the main cabin door for balance. Usually, she pulled her hair back into a ponytail before starting the day, but this morning had been hectic and chaotic. Her brother had died, and she was struggling to come to terms with the reality of it. She couldn't handle losing her only son as well. *Jesus*, she thought. The sun was relentless, heating the exterior of Winnie to a least 120 degrees, scorching the palm of her hand. "Please, honey, it's blistering hot out here!" she pleaded, submitting to the hurricane-like conditions, minus the rain. Zac's 175-pound frame shook Winnie as he approached the door.

Gripping the handle, he could feel the strong winds attempting to rip the door off its hinges. "Come on in," he said, firmly holding the thin door, preventing the weather from claiming another victim.

"Zachary, I'm so sorry, baby!" she said, as tears reacquainted her bloodshot eyes.

Zac too began to tear up; he could feel his face swelling. The feeling of a band tightening around his head caused a splitting headache. He couldn't speak, his mouth was bone-dry, as if he had eaten a pound of sand without quenching his thirst. Janis forced him into her arms. Her normal morning breeze-scented perfume was absent. Replaced with the smell of someone that hadn't yet bathed for the day. "What happened?" he asked.

Janis stumbled over her words, "Jimmy was telling us about his plan to take you to Kanas City tomorrow, and Rick got upset. Typical. Jimmy tried to calm him down, but that only escalated the situation.

Rick pushed him, not hard, I think it was to get his attention is all," she explained.

"Why the hell would he push him!?" Zac asked as sadness replaced itself with boiling rage.

"He was mad, baby," she said, in an almost defensive tone.

Zac wiped his eyes. "I don't get it, Mom—why him? Why Uncle J!?" There was a brief silence. Zac wondered, *was he sick and we didn't know?*

"I don't have that answer, honey. I wish I did." Janis sat on the sofa. "Here, sit, baby," she said, patting the middle cushion twice.

Zac sat, his head resting in his hands. His sharp elbows dug into the indention slightly above each knee cap, slowing putting his legs to sleep. Tucking his overgrown hair behind his left ear, he turned slightly to face his mother. "He was taking me to Kansas City tomorrow," he said, trying to prevent his thin, bottom lip from quivering.

"I know, he told me," she replied.

"I'm going to Kansas City, Mom!"

A bewildered look quickly filled her face. "Baby, I'm not sure that's a good idea. What about the funeral and everything?"

The thought of a funeral never crossed his mind. Zac filled the dead air as fast as he could, "We're only going to be gone a couple days. I'll be back for that," he responded.

"We?" she asked.

Zac felt an interrogation coming. "Mel, Jax, Double, and I think Alicia and Paul are coming too."

The idea of his friends tagging along did little to prevent red flags from embedding themselves into her brain.

He continued, "Mom, I have to go. I have to know why."

She could tell this was one of many firsts. Zac was a man now, she could merely advise, directing was obsolete. "You don't even know where in Kanas City he was taking you."

Zac stood, pins and needles shot up his legs, he could barely put pressure on them as hobbled to the table. He recovered the white index card. "I found this in his Rolodex," he said, handing the index card to her.

She briefly scanned the name and address, "Who's Tiny?"

Zac shrugged. "No idea, but that's the only contact in his Rolodex with a Kanas City address, so I figured we'd start there."

She looked at the card again, thinking she might have missed a clue or something that would help identify the mystery man, or woman. "What about money? And how will you get there?" He hurried to the sex den, returning with a sheet of paper in his hand. "I also found this," he said, handing her the document.

Her eyes began to tear up again as she gasped for air, holding her left hand to her mouth.

"He left everything to me, Mom, so we are taking this, and I have money saved from working this summer, as does everyone else," he said, feeling like he dodged a bullet as she scanned Jimmy's will. Zac wasn't about to tell her about the cash he'd discovered. He knew she would tell Rick, and then all hell would break loose, with him trying to break into Winnie with the hope of padding his dwindling checking and savings accounts.

"What should we say to Rick?" she asked.

Zac didn't mention it; however, the exact thought had been bouncing around in his head since he and his friends had devised their plan to road trip six hours north to a city he had never visited. To him, there was only one option. "I'm not telling him a thing, Mom. I understand he is your husband, so you can tell him if you'd like. But I have nothing to say to that man."

She looked up to the ceiling, not knowing how to respond. "Okay, baby. When are you guys planning on taking off?"

He looked her in the eyes. "Tomorrow—early," he said, bracing himself for what was to come. A statement of disapproval was sure to follow.

"Zachary!" she shouted, arching her shoulders, sitting abruptly upright.

Zac continued to lay his plan out. Promising to call, keeping her abreast on his location and safety, knowing his mother would expect nothing less.

Janis placed her hand on his leg as he returned to the sofa, "Promise me you'll be safe. I know you're 18 now, but you're still my baby."

It was a valid request, and Zac had no issue abiding by her wishes.

Janis stood and started for the door after handing the will back to Zac.

"Hey, Mom…" Zac said, stopping her in her tracks.

She slowly turned around. "Yes, dear?"

Zac's frown turned upside-down as a smile replaced it. "Thought you might like to know, Mel and I are a couple now. I asked her out last night."

She instantly placed her hands over her heart; she was euphoric.

Melany turned around and waved goodbye to Alicia before stepping into her house. The two of them had turned in their resignations to Ms. Cleveland. Who, surprisingly, was cool with them not providing her with a two weeks' notice. Melany was positive Ms. Cleveland was going to lecture them on how irresponsible it was not to give an employer notice before leaving, but they were met with zero resistance. Ms. Cleveland even asked them to pass on her condolence to Zac for his loss. Melany still felt guilty for her actions, though; she knew they were completely out character for her. However, what Melany didn't realize was that Ms. Cleveland's prayers had been answered. Last night, she had begged God to somehow get her out of her current predicament with Jax, as she was certain Zac, Melany, and Alicia knew her dirty little secret. A secret she prayed wouldn't come back to haunt her. Now that all three of them were out of the picture, she felt a great deal of relief. She even informed both girls that she would be more than willing to provide them with a solid reference should they need it for future employment.

"Stay (I Missed You)" by Lisa Loeb & Nine Stories was announced #1 for the week and playing on the radio as Melany stood next to her neatly made bed deep in thought. Hearing the broadcast snapped her out of her trance-like state as she became elated that she'd included the song on the mixtape she'd made for the road trip. Tapping the tape against her cheek, she smiled, thinking how much Zac would enjoy the compilation of songs she'd put together. She walked across her pink-shag rug to retrieve a black permanent marker from inside the top drawer of her nightstand. The pleasant scent of mulberry became stronger as she placed the tape next to the burning candle. Firmly holding the tape down, she wrote *Road Trip '94* on the blank white sticker; flapping it like a Polaroid photograph until the ink dried. Excitement raced through her body as she zipped up her bag and headed for the door. This was her first road trip without her parents tagging along, and she was going with the man of her dreams. Heading out, she felt a huge sense of accomplishment: she had managed to invite Alicia, clear the trip with her folks, inform Ms. Cleveland most of her guards quit, and pack—all in four hours.

Melany's mom parked right behind Winnie. Melany said, "That's what we're taking," pointing to the Winnebago.

Her mom noticed the dancing dead bears and turned to her, "Melany, are you sure about this?!" Melany flashed her pearly-whites, "Mom, it will be fine. You know everyone, and I'll call you every stop. If you need me, page me, and I'll have them pull over." Her mom wasn't concerned about who she was going with, her hesitation had more to do with the size of the RV. She knew none of them had ever driven anything as massive, "Who's driving this thing?"

Melany fumbled her words, "Zac said his uncle let him drive it around, and Paul's parents have one as well." She prayed her response would dilute her mothers' reluctance. "Please be safe, honey!"

Melany hugged her, "I will mom—promise!"

CHAPTER 14

He's My Pass

Zac opened the door, Melany couldn't have looked more beautiful standing on the steps. The setting sun caught her blueish-green eyes, giving them an ethereal glow as she stood before him. A butterfly conservatory took residence in his stomach. "Come in, my lady," he said, bowing while holding out his arm. Once inside, he pulled her close.

She placed her forehead against his, "Can you feel that?" she asked, referring to the energy that passed fervently through her body. Their bodies seemed to melt together.

"I've never felt anything like it before," he replied, standing in the middle of the main living area, no words were spoken as they embraced their magnetic connection.

A thump intruded from their left.

"What was that?" she asked.

Zac turned. "I think it was my controller."

They stepped into the sex den to investigate. The Super Nintendo's player-one controller was lying on the floor. "Yep, it was on the bed," he said laughing.

Melany picked the controller up and looked at the TV. "Tetris—huh?"

Zac attempted to pry the controller from her grasp. "Guilty—give it here!"

She used her butt and back to box him out. "I got $10 says I can kick your ass!" she proclaimed.

"Girl—you know I don't need your money. I'm a baller now!" The tussle was a welcome distraction; the thought of losing Uncle J was absent—at least momentarily.

Zac fetched another controller from under the TV stand.

Melany sat beside him, scanning the sex den, in awe of the decor. Her attention fixated on the CD player. "Hey—does Uncle J have a CD case?" She looked at Zac, realizing her question made it sound like his uncle were still here. He didn't appear to notice, he pressed on, setting up the game for two.

"He does—underneath there," he replied, pointing to the cabinet under the radio.

Melany located the CDs. "Holy shit, this is huge!"

Zac couldn't' refrain, "That's what she said."

Melany gave him "the eye."

Zac became bright-eyed, eyebrows raised. "Got it—that's where we draw the line."

Melany flipped through the CDs, each sleeve contained the artists cover work, along with their CD. Uncle J had the case alphabetically organized by genre, the first being *rock*. She turned page after page. Melany's cheeks dimpled. "Yes!" she said, then lifted the lid and placed her selection in the player.

They laid on their stomachs, feet in the air at the head of the bed; their sandals fell off their feet.

Controller in tote, "I'm the first player!" Melany declared.

Zac figured fighting her was pointless, quickly forfeiting by handing over the controller. They gazed hypnotically at the television screen as "Once" by Pearl Jam echoed through Winnie's surround sound, matching tile-after-tile.

Zac nudged her shoulder, "*Pearl Jam*—huh?"

She winked. Melany paused the game, moved to her side, facing Zac, "I suppose now is as good of a time as any…Zac, I'm in love with Eddie Vedder. You need to know that if I ever meet him, he's my pass."

Zac grinned. "Does that mean I get a pass, too?"

Jealousy engulfed her, instantly regretting the comment. She hadn't imagined Zac with anyone but her. She hesitantly investigated, "Who's your pass?"

Zac turned to his side to face her, rubbing his chin as if he was suddenly rooted in deliberation. "Joey Lauren Adams!"

Melany looked shocked. "From *Dazed and Confused*?"

"Hell yeah—she's freakin' hot!"

Melany, wearing her poker face, held out her hand to shake Zac's, "Deal!"

Zac cocked his head. Spidey-sense on full alert. "Really!?"

Melany returned her focus to the game. "Sure—like you're ever gonna meet that bitch!" Level four had been cleared.

Zac glared to his left in Melany's direction. He slowly bumped his foot against hers, hoping the action would be reciprocated.

Melany's tan, silky, freshly-shaved leg greeted his as she slid them up and down his calf.

Zac turned to his side, longing to kiss her lips. His heart pounded trying to escape its cage. The release of melanin had blessed her with beautiful patches of freckles that stretched across her face, mostly from months of sun exposer at the pool. The scent of her perfume flooded the room with the fresh fragrance of woodsy citrus. Her soft, luscious lips touched his gently, but briefly, as she pulled him close. They teased each other, heads together, transferring their energy to one another. "I can feel you," she whispered, referring to his soul.

Zac felt it too—she was his Yin and him her Yang.

He flexed his arms, running them up and down her back as he moved to kiss her neck. He ran his hands through her locks of dark hair, firmly gripping a handful.

"My God!" she moaned. Pushing him onto his back, she climbed on top of him. Their pelvic bones acquainted themselves for the first time.

Zac could feel her getting wet through her thin, biker shorts. His erection pulsated as she pressed herself against it. He prayed to himself, *please don't cum, please don't cum.*

Melany looked deeply into his eyes, "Zachary, how many girls have you been with?"

Valid question, inopportune time, he thought. Zac hoped to avoid the inquiry, terrified to divulge the answer. Unlike his friends, he was a virgin. He'd had opportunities, yet, somehow, he always knew Melany was the one. "Zero, I've never had sex," he said.

Melany began to glow, her eyes twinkled.

"What?" he asked.

She placed her hands on his chest. "Don't be embarrassed, I'm a virgin too!"

A calm came over him, "What about Chad? You dated him all of our sophomore year."

"I know, and he tried, but it never felt right."

Zac appeared amused—his voice dropped an octave, "Does it feel right now?"

There was a brief silence. "Nothing has ever felt more right," she whispered in his ear.

CHAPTER 15

THE LAST CHARGE

The night passed quickly. Zac laid on his back as Melany sprawled out on his chest, fast asleep, while he gazed at the ceiling thinking, *fucking sex den.* He had played the scenario out in his mind for years, yet, the thought of Uncle J playing a supporting role had never crossed his mind. Even so, this was, by far, better than anything he could have imagined; she was indeed his person.

Honk! Melany woke. "What the fuck was that!?" she asked.

Zac laughed. "Jax!"

Melany scrambled to find her clothes.

Zac put on his t-shirt and shorts. "What do you want me to say?"

Melany's face was blank. "Hell, I don't know!"

Zac instructed her to hang back. "I got this," he said, walking into the living area. He took a deep breath and walked into the step well to answer the door.

Zac heard Jax talking to Double. *Shit,* he thought, desperately trying to figure out how he could get them to leave, at least long enough to give Melany a chance to escape their predicament. Bam! Bam! Zac turned toward the door. *That mother-fucker!* he thought, stepping to open the door. Jax stood on the step, eager to enter. Standing in the stairwell, Zac stood above them, "What up, Paul," he said—not expecting them all so soon, as the three waited impatiently to come inside.

Jax was the first to enter. "Fuck the pleasantries—why the fuck are you glowing!?"

Zac froze. "Um—I'm not glowing." It was the best he could do.

Jax stood inches from his face. Zac could smell stale cigarettes on his breath. "You're glowing!"

Winnie sunk to the left as Double and Paul entered.

Paul stepped next to Jax to examine Zac. "Yeah, this mother-fucker had him some sex—I can smell pussy a mile away." Paul's southern drawl made his comment even funnier. That, and because, to the best of his knowledge, he didn't know about Melany yet.

They probed Zac for answers. "Now, who you been fuckin?" Paul asked, poking him in the chest.

Zac smiled. "You guys are fucking nuts. I chilled last night." Lying wasn't Zac's forte, an attribute they all knew he did not possess.

Standing motionless, they scoured the RV, looking for any evidence of a close sexual encounter.

"Z, this place is awesome!" Paul said, adding, "and I'm so sorry for your loss, bro. Uncle J was a legend."

Zac's head sank a bit. "Thanks, man. I miss him a lot."

Winnie shook in the rear.

Double interrupted, "What the fuck was that?!"

Zac stomped his foot hard on the floor, adding to Winnie's swaying, "It does that all the time—tires must be low."

Jax flipped Zac off and headed to the sex den. Double and Paul followed close behind, like detectives about to unmask the culprit.

"Stop, there's nothing back there!" Zac stated.

Jax slid the partition to the left. Double and Paul peered over his shoulders.

"Heyyyyyy!" Melany said, standing in her bra and matching panties. Her face squinting, eyebrows raised, she snatched the blanket off the bed and wrapped around her in one swift motion.

Their eyes widened and jaws dropped. "Fuck me! Z nubbed Mel!" Paul shouted.

Melany's face turned beet red.

Jax and Double cried with laughter.

Jax turned to Zac, "You dirty bastard! Nailed the hottest chick in school. You're a God, Z!"

Zac felt like he stood an inch or two taller, overjoyed.

Double killed the moment, "Mel, was he any good?"

She didn't say a word.

"What the fuck, Double—who asks shit like that?" Zac said.

"What? You know, enquiring minds what to know—bitch!" Double added.

"He was the best I've ever had!" Mel yelled.

They cheered and yelled, "Dog-pile!" pulling Melany down onto the bed.

Zac thought, *Fuck—I hope she's fastened her bra!*

Jax was the last to load his bag inside. "Let's do this, bitches!" he hollered.

Melany stepped into the living area. "Yeah…about that," she said.

Double and Paul sat smiling at the brick of weed resting in front of them.

Paul punched Jax' leg with his nub and whispered, "This shit is about to get good, son."

Jax faced Zac. "What the fuck, dude, spit it out, you know I hate suspense." His arms stretched like Michael Jordan's "Wings" poster.

Zac didn't have a say in the matter, nor did he care, "Mel invited Leesh man, and she said she'd love to come," Zac said, waiting for the explosion.

A wave of rage flowed through Jax. "Oh—hell no! Fuck no, man!"

Zac attempted to calm him down. "It's all good, man, chill. She's going to be kicking it with Mel." Zac's attempt fell on cold ears.

It wasn't that Jax didn't like Alicia; he was embarrassed—something he'd never cough up to. Calmly, Jax said, "Alright, man, whatever! But for the record, I object!"

Alicia's Ford Probe turned the corner and parked behind the boat. She stepped out wearing a white tank top, black running shorts, and sandals. Jax watched her approach Winnie. She looked like a movie star walking toward them, her hair blowing slowly in the wind, "Fuck me," Jax whispered.

Zac stood behind him. "It will be fine, man. Besides, I don't have a ping-pong table in this thing."

Jax punched him in the dick. "Fuck you, Z!"

Stepping into Winnie, Alicia's perfume filled the living area with the sweet scent of Jasmine. Like everyone else who entered, she stood mesmerized by the Grateful Dead décor. Zac welcomed her aboard.

"Z, I'm so sorry for your loss. Uncle J was the coolest adult I've ever met. How are you doing?"

Zac felt her soft-spoken condolences to be genuine, "Thanks Leesh. I'm as good as I can be—thanks for asking. Let me get that for you." He snatched her duffel bag.

Double and Paul acknowledged her, "What up, Leesh!"

She smiled. "Hey guys—is that!?" The brick of weed had shocked her, as it had everyone.

"Indeed it is, darlin'—indeed, it is," Paul said.

She bent over to smell it. "My God! Is it as good as it smells?"

Double had been rolling joint after joint since he had sat down. "No clue, rolling these for the trip," Double said, licking the rolling paper like an envelope.

Reluctantly, Jax, who was grabbing a pop from the fridge, also welcomed her, "Hey, Leesh."

She blushed. "Hi, Jax."

Doubled briefly stopped rolling and looked at his wrist. "Z, its 11, bro. If we're going to get there before 6, we gots to roll!"

Zac agreed.

Paul stood up. "You want me to man-handle this bitch, Z?"

Zac was relieved. He hadn't told anyone, but driving Winnie scared the shit out of him. He was used to driving a VW Rabbit. "Yeah, man—if you don't mind."

Paul reached into his bag on the sofa, grabbed his eight-ball steering wheel grip aid, jumped in the captain's chair, and affixed it to the wheel. Because of his disability, Paul used the eight-ball to assist him in making turns—a pretty fucking cool invention if you ask him.

Zac reached to his waist, "Fuck!" he said.

"What is it?" Melany asked, stroking his shoulder.

Zac reached for the doorknob. "Hold up a second, Paul. I forgot my pager on my dresser. I'll be right back." He sprinted to his room. It was quiet, both Janis and Rick had left hours ago for work, and he wanted to get out of town before they came home for lunch. His pager was where he left it, next to his CD player on the dresser. Zac looked at the display—no new pages, then strapped it to his shorts waistband. Walking toward the end of the hallway, he paused. He could still smell his uncles' aftershave. A tear slipped down his cheek. "I love you, Uncle J!" he said to the empty room.

Zac closed the apartment door behind him, wiping away his tears before turning around.

"Why the fuck are all those cars parked back here?"

The question came from a voice Zac did not want to hear. *This mother-fucker doesn't even have the Goddamn common courtesy to pay me his condolences.* "My friends are here." he said to Rick as he walked past him, intentionally throwing his shoulder into Rick's.

Zac's crew heard Rick's voice, shuffling to the windows of Winnie to catch a glimpse of what was happening.

"Where the hell do you think you're going!?" Rick demanded.

Zac continued walking. "That's none of your damn business!"

Rick grabbed Zac's arm, violently spinning him around.

"What the fuck, man!" Zac yelled.

Rick got right up into his face.

Zac looked down at him, balling his hands into fists.

"Oh, you're a tough guy now, huh?!" Rick said, looking up to his stepson. "Well, what are you going to do, tough guy!?" Rick pushed him, not hard, but he had Zac's attention.

Zac stepped forward, towering over his elder, "Don't you ever fucking touch me again!"

Rick could feel Zac's heavy breath on his face as it exited his nostrils. "Your mother said you're planning on taking a trip in that thing—that shit ain't happening while you live under my roof."

Zac smirked at Rick, turning to face him. "I don't live in this shit hole anymore. I've got my own place." He turned to leave.

Rick grabbed his arm again. "I said you're not going anywhere, boy!"

Zac was losing control—his mind went blank.

"Zac, come on!" Melany yelled from the cabin door, "it's not worth it!" she added.

Zac glanced at her. She appeared scared.

Rick pushed Zac from behind, making him stumble forward. Without thinking, Zac violently swung around and clocked Rick square in the jaw.

Rick stumbled backward, landing in the grass.

Pain radiated in Zac's right hand. "Fuck-en-A!" Zac yelled, holding his hand in his lap. He had never hit anyone. The pain briefly dissolved as adrenaline shot to his soul. He ran and jumped into the front seat of Winnie.

Melany quickly slammed and locked the cabin door.

Rick jumped to his feet. "Get your ass back here, boy!" he screamed, holding his jaw.

Zac slid the passenger window open—sticking his head out, "Fuck you and your shitty apartment, you lame-ass, movie-quoting, mother-fucker!" Zac looked to Paul, "Go!"

CHAPTER 16

27

Rick disappeared from the side-door mirror as they turned onto the road heading toward the I-35 North onramp enroute to Kanas City.

Double punched Zac's arm. "That shit was gangster, Z! You knocked that punk-ass out!"

Zac tuned toward Double with a broad smile. "That felt so good!" he declared.

Melany sat on the sofa behind Paul, biting her bottom lip while staring at her man.

Zac caught the look, adrenaline passed, arousal took its place. She looked sexy as hell with one leg propped on the sofa, showing enough skin to make things move downstairs. Zac wanted her, and bad. However, that would have to wait.

Jax walked to the front of Winnie. "How's the hand, Ali?" he said, handing Zac a bag of frozen peas he'd retrieved from the freezer.

Zac placed the peas on his hand to get ahead of the swelling. "I can move it, so must not be broken—thank God!" he said, repeatedly making a fist with little-to-no difficulty.

Melany piped up, "I put something together for the trip," she said, inserting her compilation of songs into the tape player.

The crew sat in anticipation, curious as to what her first song would be. Fats Domino's "Kanas City" roared through the speakers. Winnie shook side-to-side, flying down to interstate as everyone sang and danced in unison.

"Oh—yeah! We can dance, and drive! How many times can you say you did that!?" Alicia said, backing her ass into Double's. Everyone danced that much more. Double even did the *Running Man* in front of the sofa—lifting his legs to his waist, one at a time, while moving his arms methodically up and down, as fast they'd permit.

Melany returned to her seat, enjoying her friends' happiness, and thought, *nailed it!*

Two hours down the road, they stopped to fill up the gas tank. Paul asked, "Anyone else want to drive? I'm beat!"

Jax shouted from the back, "I got you, my Caucasian."

Zac stepped into the galley, passing Jax who was heading to the captain's chair. "You sure, bro?" Zac asked, hesitant to let him drive.

Jax sat. "Dude, I drive a boat—I got this."

Zac laid down, placing his head on Melany's lap as she began to run her hands through his hair. Zac looked up at Melany smiling, "Watch this…No fucking Beatles!"

Melany snort laughed.

Double grabbed his duffle-bag from behind his seat at the table. There was a baseball bat on top secured by its handles.

Paul took the chair across from him at the table as he had before. Paul's nose wrinkled; the space between his eyebrows bulged. "Why the did you bring a fucking baseball bat?"

Everyone else had been curious as well.

Double, firmly holding the padded grip, informed them, "Well, I don't own a gun, and I'm certain none of you law-abiding citizens brought anything to protect us. I thought ol' Betsy here would do just fine!"

They all laughed at the look on his smiling face, suggesting he was ready to lay someone out.

"Let me see that thing," Paul said, reaching for the bat.

Double moved it out of his reach. "Sorry, bro, this here is a left-handed bat."

Paul pouted. "Oh."

The rest of the crew attempted to wrap their heads around Double's statement.

Jax looked back at Paul in the rearview mirror. "Ha—you dumbass! There is no such thing as a left-handed bat—that's rich!"

Paul sulked. "Fuck you, Jax!" he said.

Mile markers passed as fast as they came. A warm breeze wrapped around Jax as he passed a road sign that read: Kanas City 107.

"This seat taken?" Alicia asked, rhetorically.

"Um—no, sit." Jax didn't know what to say. The last time they'd spoke, he'd bolted out of her house, never returning her pages or calls. They sat in silence as the minutes passed.

Alicia began to sing softly, "Love Me Do" by The Beatles.

Jax attention was captured. He thought he heard his second favorite Beatles song exiting her mouth. "What are you singing over there?" he queried, cupping his hand around his ear. "I was listening to "Love Me Do" on my way to Z's place," Jax wrinkled his forehead in disbelief. "You're a *Beatles* fan? How did I not know this?"

Her perfect smile, shadowed only by her breathtaking appearance, widened. "Do I have tits!?"

Jax investigated, moving his eyes to her perky breasts. "

"Really!?"

"Ok, pop quiz! How many number one hits have they had all together?" Jax asked, convinced she wouldn't know the answer.

Alicia confidently answered, "27!"

Jax fake laughed her. "That's what I thought. You were trying to ease the tension between us by claiming to be a fan—they had 17!" He turned his attention back to the interstate.

Alicia, still gazing in his direction, wasn't finished with the conversation. "You asked how many number ones they had *all together*, right? Well, for your information, mister fucking *Beatles lover.* They had 17 singles hit number one in the U.S. and 10 that hit number one in England. Which, if I did my math correctly, they had," she leaned over the armrest, facing the rear, "Mike, can you please tell me what 17 plus 10 is?"

Double looked baffled, hitting a joint, prematurely exhaling, "Uhh—27?"

She rejoiced and face forward. "Thanks, dear!"

Jax jaw fell to the floor, "Love me do! Like, really, love me do!" he said, reaching out his hand toward hers.

She looked at his hand as it hovered over the console, feeling victorious, "Aww—I love me do, too, Jax," she said, firmly gripping his hand."

Unbeknownst to him, he'd soon find his womanizing ways behind him. From that moment forward, the two were inseparable.

CHAPTER 17

Tiny's Place

The Kansas City skyline was an instant reminder that Zac and friends were not in Oklahoma anymore. Massive skyscrapers cast shade on the city as the sun set for the day. Zac sat between Jax and Alicia on the console with Melany, Double, and Paul hovering above. Each excited with curiosity of what adventures lay ahead. Their eyes marveled at the collection of high-rise buildings that had seemingly burst out of nowhere in the center of the town. Oklahoma City had a few tall buildings, but nothing that compared to what towered ahead of them.

With stops, they entered city limits eight hours after departing Weatherford, missing their goal of arriving by six. The map Uncle J gifted Zac did little in providing them directions to Tiny's Place. The map broke down the major highways and interstates, not the city streets.

"Hey, pull off the next exit and stop at the nearest gas station. I'll see if they have a map of the city," Zac said.

Jax drove into the heart of the city before finding an exit that looked somewhat safe for young outsiders.

The first gas station they came to had a quaint, mom-and-pop shop feel to it. The bright green tiled roof with the slogan *Big Jack's Bar-B-Que* displayed across it, helped calm their nerves because it closely resembled a bar-b-que shack in Oklahoma City they frequented. Jax pulled up to the gas pump to top off.

"Alright, I'll run inside and see if they have a map," Zac said, kissing Melany before his departing dismount. As he pulled the handprint-stained door open a bell chimed. The aroma of slow-smoked meats greeted him. There was three aisles separating the gas station from Big Jack's Barbeque restaurant in the back. Zac walked down the middle aisle only to find the same map he already possessed. *Shit,* he thought, feeling somewhat defeated. Unable to accept defeat, he went to the front counter to ask for assistance.

Approaching the counter, Zac noticed a large, middle-aged, black man standing close to 6' 7" tall behind the counter. His head was bald, and Zac could only see his white t-shirt behind his faded, stained—bar-b-que sauce if he had to guess—apron, sans nametag. As Zac inched closer, the man bore a striking resemblance to Hightower from the movie *Police Academy*. His toneless lisp welcomed Zac. He even had a large gap between his teeth. The man asked, "How can I help you, young man?"

"Um, yes, sir…I need a map of the city. Do you have any?"

The man walked to the end of the counter to a rack displaying postcards of local attractions. He handed Zac a map. "Where you headed?" he said as he returned to the register.

Zac looked up to him. "Chandler Street. You ever hear of it?"

"Oh-hell, son. You don't need a map to get to Chandler Street. It's right down the road!" The man continued, "But what business you got down there? Ain't no houses. That there is a business district."

Zac was confused. He was certain Tiny's address would be a residence, not a business.

The man questioned Zac again, "Who you looking for? I'm sure I know them."

Zac pulled the index card from his right side pocket and handed it to the man.

He smiled, "Shit, boy—Tiny's joint isn't but three block from here! I go there all the time."

Zac's confusion persisted. "Tiny's joint?" Zac asked.

"His joint—you know, his bar." The man returned the index card, and Zac stowed it back into his pocket. "Can you give me directions?"

The man smiled, "Absolutely! You here for the contest?"

Zac didn't have to ask, his face said it all.

The man laughed and went on to inform him that Tiny's Place was home to the "Forever Music Contest" held every second Tuesday of the month. An event that drew the best acts Missouri had to offer. It also attracted some big names in the industry, and with a purse of a thousand bucks, contestants figured entering was a no-brainer.

Zac headed for the door. "Thanks for the info and directions, sir!"

The man nodded. "Hey, son—a tip. Don't stare!"

Zac held the map up, silently thanking him as he thought, *what the does that mean?*

The crew was outside stretching. "I got it. It's a bar!" Zac said.

Jax interjected, "Fuck yes! This trip is going to be sick!" He and Double exchanged a handshake to celebrate.

Zac stepped inside, "Where's Paul?"

Melany stood on the steps and pointed to the payphones near the bathroom. "He said he needed to call his parents."

They all piled in and waited.

The cabin door opened, Paul stood in the step well, his face blotchy, like he'd watched Bambi's mother die, a second time.

Melany jumped from the sofa. She placed a concerned arm around him for comfort. "Paul, what's wrong?" she probed.

Everyone waited anxiously to find out what was troubling him.

He tried to find his voice, "Byron—he—he was in a tractor accident. My dad said he was pulling a stump out of the ground and he had it in too high of a gear. He said the chains popped off, hitting him in the head. Byron suffered a horrific head injury."

Zac stood with them in the galley. "Dude, is he going to be okay? Do we need to go back?"

Paul's cry's became violent, "He's going into surgery now!"

Zac looked at Jax and pointed to the captain's chair, "Get us back onto the interstate—we're going home!"

Paul stopped. "No, he's going to be fine! The doctor said he needs a prosthetic head."

Zac and Melany took a step back.

Double muttered, "What the fuck?!"

Jax turned around, hung over the armrest, and asked, in a serious tone, "They make those?"

Melany pushed Paul as hard as she could in the chest as he began to die laughing. "No, fuck-stick—they don't make those. Who's the dumbass now!?"

Jax faced the front. Winnie had been running the moment after Zac rejoined the crew. With everyone standing, he slammed the gas, launching his friends airborne. "You're an asshole!" Jax yelled.

Pulling into Tiny's, the massive parking lot was nearly empty, except for a reasonably-new, jet black Ford Mustang, and a white Isuzu Rodeo parked next to three empty handicap spaces. Jax parked underneath an oak tree along a broken down, red-stained wooden fence. "What is with "famous" barbecue in this city?" Jax asked, looking up to an orange neon sign that read: Tiny's Famous Bar and Bar-B-Que.

Fair question. Almost every store or gas station seemed to sell the most "famous" barbecue the city had to offer.

"Henry Perry is from Kansas City, fool," Double said.

Jax turned off the ignition and faced Double, "Who the hell is Henry Perry?"

Double explained that Henry Perry was the "father of Kansas City barbecue," and that in the early 1900s, he would walk around selling the meat he prepared after wrapping it in newspaper.

Everyone stared.

"How in the hell do you know that?!" Paul asked.

Double sat shock at the ignorance of his closest friends, "I like to read!"

Zac opened the heavy, dark, wood door for Melany, closely following behind, along with the crew. It was dimly lit, not a soul was to be found. They stood in the entryway. Shocked by the rock 'n' roll décor, Jax pointed to the bar. Images of The Beatles canvased the wall behind the bar. Huge wooden whiskey barrels acted as spouts for beer taps. The wall leading to the restrooms had Pink Floyd *The Wall* painted up and down a light gray cement wall background, with pictures hung throughout. Each one portraying a little person partying with famous musicians.

Zac noticed one picture of a small man with Uncle J. He and Jerry Garcia held the small man as he laid across their arms. Reminding Zac of a disturbing photo he'd seen of Burt Reynolds Nude on a Bear Skin

Rug. He shuddered the memory away then laughed. The little man and Uncle J looked to be in their late 20s or early 30s. He wore his hair curly and long, to his shoulders, and, like his uncle, wore a Grateful Dead t-shirt, board shorts, and sandals. "Do you know him, Zac?" Alicia asked, looking at the photo.

"No. I've never even heard of him," Zac replied, quickly swiping a tear from his left eye before it rolled down his cheek.

Around the corner, a high-pitched voice shouted from across the room. Everyone turned. An older version of the small man in the photos briskly walked passed a large stage in their direction, "What the hell are you kids doing in here?!" the little man shouted, waving his small fist at them.

Zac turned to Jax. The "*don't stare*" comment from the man at the gas station came to mind in an instant. Zac's hand reached out in slow motion as he noticed Jax's eyes squinting as the edge of his lips curved into a Joker-like grin. Jax' right arm raised, pointing at the small man, "Holy shit! It's *Willow*!" exited his mouth before Zac could react.

The small man fumed, "What the hell did you call me!?"

Zac jumped between the man and his friend. "I'm sorry, sir! We recently found out my friend here is a dumbass!" Zac said.

Everyone but Jax laughed.

The small man asked, "Why are you in my bar, kid?"

Zac looked at his friends, "Can you guys give us a second?"

They walked past Zac and the small man. "We'll be sitting over there," Melany said, pointing near the stage.

The small man looked up to Zac. "Kid, you better start talking, or I'm calling the cops!"

Zac made eye contact with the man. His voice went a bit horse, "Mr. I'm Zac Taylor. Jimmy Taylor's nephew."

The small man opened his arms. His fuming face changed to one of a grown man beaming with happiness. "Well, I'll be damned! You guys made it! Where is that old bastard!?" he said, looking behind him, waiting for Uncle J to enter the bar at any moment. Not finding him, the small man grew impatient. "Wait a second, why are they here?" he asked, pointing to Zac's friends.

Tears crept into Zac's eyes as the man turned. Zac's body language said it all.

"No! Don't tell me!" he said.

Zac shook his head, confirming the horrible news.

CHAPTER 18

WHY KANSAS CITY?

The small man hopped up onto a bar stool, (that Zac considered, "a custom" piece of furniture for a man of his stature), instructing Zac to have a seat next to him.

Zac struggled to tell him about Uncle J. He hadn't had much time to mourn with all the events that had transpired within the past two days. The small man began to fall apart upon hearing the details. However, he took comfort in knowing Zac had laid Rick out in his backyard. Zac asked the small man hesitantly, "Sir, I'm sorry, but who are you? Uncle J never told me he was friends with a little person. The small man belly-laughed, "Zac, you know me. Your uncle probably referred to me as Arlo."

Zac was more than familiar with the name. Uncle J had told him countless stories about a man named Arlo. A man that followed the Dead with him, selling alcoholic beverages by his side for years. Zac cried, "You're Arlo Winston!?"

Arlo held his arm out and bowed his head, "He, be-ith, I."

Zac reached out his hand to shake Arlo's; a gesture he returned. Zac found himself staring at Arlo's hand in his palm. It seemed fragile, and Zac's hand swallowed it—almost to the point his hand wasn't visible.

Arlo noticed. This wasn't the first time someone had done the same. Arlo's voice startled Zac, "You know, Jimmy was the only person to see me as a man and not a small person. He made me feel comfortable with who I am as an individual. That's something no one has ever done in my 50 years on this Earth."

Zac smiled. That sounded like Uncle J. He had always preached that one should treat everyone, regardless of their differences, with kindness and respect.

Arlo explained that he had met Uncle J at a Dead show in San Francisco. Jimmy's booth was set up across from his at that particular show, and he had caught Jimmy staring at him off and on throughout the afternoon. Not a creepy kind of stare, but the kind where one wants to fixate on something they weren't accustomed to seeing on a daily basis. When the band began to play, and business died down, Jimmy walked over to Arlo's booth. He didn't introduce himself, he simply said, "I'm going to ask you a series of questions, and I want you to say "addicted" after each one. Arlo found it to be a bit odd, but decided to play along:

Jimmy: People that use crack are…

Arlo: Addicted

Jimmy: Compulsive gamblers gamble because they are…

Arlo: Addicted

Jimmy: What hit you on the side of your face last night?

Arlo: Addicted

Zac laughed at the story. His uncle had used it on him once as well.

Zac was awe-struck to hear some of the same stories he had from his uncle, but this time it was from someone else's perspective.

Arlo paused, "How did you know to come to Kanas City, Zac?"

Zac reached into his shorts pocket, retrieving the index card he had found in the Rolodex. He passed the folded card to Arlo. "The famous Rolodex! That was smart of you," he said, returning the card.

Zac probed, "Do you know why Uncle J was bringing me here?"

Arlo sat back in the stool. "He didn't tell you?"

Zac shook his head, "No."

The two stepped down from the barstools after Arlo told Zac to follow him.

Double, Jax, and Paul were standing on the stage. Jax had a guitar strapped around his neck, as he stood at the edge of the stage, imagining he was singing to a packed house. Double was bent over reaching for the saxophone resting against a mirrored background covered in smoke-residue. Paul sat at the piano, softly tapping the keys with his nub, hitting three of them at a time. Melany and Alicia sat across from each other at a round table, center stage, talking to one another. Melany noticed Zac marching behind Arlo, and stood. Zac held up a finger, indicating he needed a second, as she mouthed *okay*.

Past the stage was the short hallway Arlo had emerged from. Zac took note of three electric guitars and three bass guitars hanging on either side of each wall. Each one signed by a famous musician. "Is that *Flea's* signature?" Zac asked, noticing his picture above the middle bass guitar.

Arlo did an about face. "It is. The Peppers performed here last year."

Zac was star struck. He ran his fingers along the strings, unable to believe a member of his favorite band had done the same.

Arlo opened the only door in the hallway. "Come in," he said, holding the door for Zac.

The office was decorated much like the bar. His dark walnut desk was cluttered with envelopes. There was a leather chair centered behind it, and three large cardboard boxes against the far wall. Each one with a different marking: XL, L, M. Above them hung a large painting of Kurt Cobain's face. His dyed, overgrown, blond hair hung below his unshaven chin as he posed expressionless, wearing his famous white sunglasses. On the wall to the left was another picture. This one of Freddy Mercury holding his outstretched microphone over what one could only assume was an enormous crowd. To the right, photos, each frame different, of the Rolling Stone's, standing behind Arlo. Zac thought, *Is there a rock star this guy hasn't met?*

Arlo asked Zac to sit while he shuffled papers in the middle drawer of the desk. "Aha—Here they are!" Arlo said. He set what he had recovered on his lap—out of Zac's line of sight, and exhaled a deeper than usual breath. Arlo then took one of what seemed like a stack of baseball cards off the top of the pile and placed it in the center of the desk. Whatever he held appeared, at least from Zac's point of view, to be bright red with perforated edges and in near mint condition. In the center, were two, one-legged, white doves perched on the neck of a blue guitar with a green headstock and tuning keys that matched the neck. It read from top to bottom:

WOODSTOCK '94

August 13th, 14th, 1994

Saugerties, New York

098535

General Admission $135.00

2 MORE

DAYS

of PEACE

& MUSIC

He explained to Zac that he and Jimmy had used their connections to obtain 10 tickets to the festival in total. Jimmy had come up with the idea of teaching Zac about peace, love, and music by giving out the unused tickets to those that wouldn't otherwise be able to afford them. That, and they knew the 25th anniversary of *Woodstock* was a once-in-a-lifetime experience, and wouldn't come around again until the 50th anniversary. Initially, they were to hit the road on the 11th; however, not too long ago they received word another day was added on the 12th—due to the enormous crowds expected. Now, they had to leave tomorrow—the 10th —to make the festival on opening day.

Zac stared at the ticket. If he heard correctly, he was going to *Woodstock '94*. He surveyed Arlo, silently asking to pick it up.

Arlo extended his arm, "Absolutely!"

The ticket was bigger than Zac's hand, and he held it delicately, like a 1989 *Upper Deck*, Ken Griffey Jr., rookie card. Zac sobbed, "But—Uncle J isn't here."

Arlo jumped down from his chair, sending the chair sliding backward, slamming into the middle cardboard box, below Cobain. He placed his hand on Zac's arm, "I know, Zac. I know. That's why you're going to take your friends!"

Zac used the back of his hand to wipe away any evidence of crying. "What do you mean, take my friends?"

Loud, muffled music began to echo down the hallway. "Sounds like the contest has begun." Arlo said, glancing toward the office door. He grabbed the stack of tickets and handed them to Zac. "There's just one catch, Zac," Arlo insisted, still holding the tickets. "You have to give the remaining tickets away to people along the way, should you have extra and come across anyone that could use the help."

Zac didn't follow, "What do you mean?"

Arlo walked to the only door in the room, and paused, "I want you to some-how, some-way, pay this opportunity forward. There are always people wanting to get into these things. They don't know how they're going to do it, they only know it's going to happen."

Zac asked, "You mean like-asking the universe?"

Arlo opened the door. "Your uncle taught you well, son. He taught you well."

CHAPTER 19

THE CONTEST

Jax stood at the end of the bar with Alicia, talking to each other over the screams of 200 plus patrons. The tables that once sat in front of the stage had been relocated, making room for the occupants. Jax noticed Zac searching for their friends from the left, waving his arms, trying to obtain his attention.

Zac stood on his toes, scanning the crowd. He located Jax at the bar, but the number of "Excuse me's," he'd had to dole out to reach him wasn't worth it.

Jax could see that his friend had been crying, even from afar. His eyes were puffy; his cheeks were swollen and red, blotchy from intermittent crying since losing Uncle J.

Zac followed Jax's pointing hand, locating Mel and friends.

Alicia pulled on Jax's shirt, "What are you doing?" she asked, barely able to hear her own voice.

Jax announced, "Z's out!"

Nine bands had already performed by the time Arlo returned to his duties as the emcee, introducing each of the remaining contestants. Jax couldn't see him, but the voice that reverberated from the speakers was too recognizable not to be the man Jax had referred to as Willow.

Alicia tried desperately to gain the bartenders attention, so she could order drinks for everyone.

Jax caught a brief glance at his friends' table in the corner. Sitting under a horizontally hung drum kit with a brass sign above it that read: "Once Played by the drummer of Metallica, Lars Ulrich." Both Melany and Zac were crying, and he could see shocked looks on Double and Paul's faces while Zac spoke to them.

The bartender was wearing a wet-spotted, blue, *Kansas City Royals* t-shirt. He stepped to Alicia as he tossed a beer cap. "What will it be, pretty lady?" he said, too busy to give a damn about her age.

Jax turned around. "Hey, my man! What's it take to get in this thing?" he said, referring to the contest. The bartender yelled, "100 bucks, friend."

Jax reached into his pocket. "Here!" he said, slamming $200 down, face up on the bar. "Give me six shots!"

A glowering Alicia stood beside Jax, "What are you doing?!" she screamed, trying to pull his arm off the bar.

Jax placed his right hand on hers, "Baby! There is only one thing that cures sadness—Music!"

The final band of the night stepped off the stage to a light round of applause after their cover of "Fall Down" by Toad the Wet Sprocket. Jax slammed a tray of shots on the table. Liquor spilled over the rims. Jax stood before them, Alicia by his side, "I want to make a toast!"

Zac thought, *Eh, what the fuck!*

Jax grabbed a shot from the tray and waited for everyone else to follow. "To lucky number 13! May the crowd favor us!" he shouted.

Zac asked over the crowd noise, "What's number 13?"

Arlo was about to announce the nights' winner. The bartender jogged to the stage. The crowd stood, waiting to hear which band would be crowned the victor. Shouts of, "*Who won?*" and *"Come on already!"* were yelled at the host as he leaned to hear the barkeeps news. Arlo held the microphone to his mouth, "Well, ladies and gentlemen. It appears we had a late, 13th entry," he said, trying to tame the boisterous crowd.

Jax looked down to his friends beaming. "Let's do this, bitches!" Jax led everyone to stage left.

A confused Arlo stood before them, trying to figure out what was going on.

Zac did the only thing he could think of with a pissed off audience grumbling behind. He held up two thumbs. They huddled.

Arlo told a corny joke to the crowd, hoping to calm them down.

Fishing for an explanation, Zac pulled Jax by the arm, "What the shit, man?!" he yelled as softly as possible.

Jax scanned his circled companions fervently. "This crying shit ends now! Uncle J would want us to celebrate him, not mourn him! He taught each of us the power of music! He showed us how it joins people regardless of the joy or tragedies we endure. And right now we're going through just that! So we're going to show these air-breathers what he showed us! Put on your big-boy pants and take your goddamn posts!"

Melany whispered, "What the hell are we going to play?"

Jax stepped away from the huddle, with his back to the crowd, "Life goes on, brah!"

Melany sat on a black, round, stool, tapping the tips of her drumsticks softly on the hanging toms, ensuring the kit was in-tune.

Alicia picked up a white, Fender, electric bass guitar, and strummed the strings, while messing with the tuning machines.

Double cleaned the mouthpiece of the saxophone he wore around his neck and took his place behind Paul.

Paul held a maraca under his left armpit while adjusting a second microphone to sing backup vocals.

Zac pulled out the stool of the Spinet piano, and stared out to the silent crowd while spotlights attempted to shadow them. Sitting down, he looked at each of his friends, nodding to each individually with confidence.

Jax faced the audience. The venue he stared upon was much different than the talent show he and a friend had won only months ago. However, the rush of adrenaline was the same, and that was all he desired: his fix.

Arlo eyed his unknown friends, noticing they seemed prepared.

Facing the crowd, Arlo realized their "band" had no name. He mumbled, struggling to craft something his observers could relate to. He glared at Zac, whose head peered over the Spinet. A calm enveloped Arlo. In Zac's eyes, he saw Jimmy. Time, in his mind, was a brief blur. Arlo felt his friend, Jimmy, standing beside him, as he did all those years ago. The words Arlo had struggled to locate, now rolled off his tongue effortlessly, "Ladies and gentlemen! I give you, *Woodstock Bound!*"

The crowd showed no change in demeanor. Stares pierced the newly-formed group.

Jax stepped to the microphone, removing a pick from the stand. He clipped the microphone into the stand's clamp, then lifted one hand in the air, pointing to the heavens, "This one's for Uncle J!" he shouted. The crowd erupted, roaring chants of, "Uncle J! Uncle J!" Instantly identifying with whom he had referred to, yet no clue of his passing.

Warm tingles swarmed Zac. He had been unaware of the influence his uncle had on so many people. He sat erect on the stool. His best friend, glaring over his left shoulder with a devilish grin, signaled to Zac to bring them in. Zac keyed in on the Spinet piano. Dun-ta-dun, dun-ta-dun, dun-ta-dun-ta bounced off the tightly-tuned piano strings. Blasting, "Ob-La-Di, Ob-La-Da," by The Beatles into the awe-struck audience. The band fell in on queue. The audience quickly identified the song, clapping after Zac's introduction.

Jax plucked his acoustic guitar strings and bellowed the song's lyrics with the crowd singing along at the top of their lungs. Jax's jubilant vocals bounced off walls of Tiny's Place.

There wasn't a sitting person in the place as Arlo stood to the right, watching his bar patrons, unknowingly, paying tribute to his fallen comrade.

The electric crowd screamed chants of *Woodstock Bound! Woodstock Bound* as Jax's band joined him, united, arm-and-arm. In a single-file line, they bowed. Screaming fans reached out, hoping to touch them. Accepting a graze of their fabric t-shirts as a consolation prize.

Hugging Zac as close as possible from the side, Jax whispered, "What's up with the *Woodstock* bit?"

Zac stared out into a pool of screaming fans, "That's why Double and Paul were crying. I told everyone Arlo gave us tickets. We're *Woodstock Bound,* baby!"

Jax threw an arm in the air, holding tightly to his guitar, and shouted with the crowd, *Woodstock Bound! Woodstock Bound!*

It was approaching one in the morning when Arlo finally met the entire crew. He had shared the same story with them as he did Zac regarding *Woodstock '94.* Sitting at the bar, Arlo in the middle, perched on his custom stool, he asked if any of them had been to a music festival before.

Alicia spoke from the end of the pack, "My parents always take me to the state fair. Does that count?"

Everyone turned to Arlo, eagerly awaiting his response.

Arlo looked to the opposite end of the bar, then slowly to back to Alicia, "This will be nothing even remotely close to a state fair. Think bigger!"

They all took the bait. His dramatic reply had raised their brows, like children believing they'd witnessed Santa Clause escaping up a chimney on Christmas Eve.

Arlo had the advantage. He not only had the experience, he had stayed abreast of all *Woodstock '94's* recent developments. He painted a picture of a vast green valley with fields of people as far as the eye could see. Two stages. The main being the North, and a smaller scale replica to the South. Multiple camera crews. Each posted three stories high in order to sell the experience to those that couldn't make the journey—via pay-per-view. Tents. Randomly pitched in the distance. No facilities to bathe. Only water fountains that cast a mist over those overheating. Naked people aimlessly strolling the grounds. Most of whom will be searching for that one thing they feel is missing in their lives: that sense of belonging to something bigger than themselves.

Paul, who was sitting to Arlo's left, placed his nub on Arlo's left arm, and stopped him, "Naked women!? Walking around!? Hell, the pretty ones can belong to me!" He had broken their trance.

"*Belong* to you," Arlo displayed a humorless smile. "Son, you have a lot to learn about women, especially the ones who listen to rock 'n' roll."

Paul shrugged.

Zac sat opposite of Paul. "Are you saying we need to get supplies? Because we don't have anything." Aware each of them had only packed for two days—at most.

Arlo grinned. "That might not be a bad idea, my friend. Also, you should get on the road first thing in the a.m. Your destination is a two-day drive, and that's *if* traffic favors you."

They each turned to one-another, chatting about what they thought they might need for the journey.

Double asked Arlo, "Is there a store we could hit up or something?"

Arlo climbed down from the stool. "There is. About five miles down the road. It will be on your way out of town."

Zac spun around, watching Arlo walk to door. "Where are you going?" he asked.

Arlo opened the entrance door. "I'm kicking you guys out. I'm tired!"

Zac led his friends out the door, holding up to inquire of Arlo, "Are you sure you don't want to join us?" he questioned with a sincere tone.

Arlo looked up with a distant expression in his eyes. "No, son. This is your adventure. Jimmy and I had ours."

CHAPTER 20

I REALLY MISS HIM

Double sat on the sofa and compiled a list of supplies needed from the General Army Navy Outlet. Everyone else hovered over the table as Zac unfolded his map to chart their course to Saugerties, New York.

"How does it look, Z?" Paul asked, staring at an upside-down North America. Zac used a bright-yellow sticky-note to help calculate how many miles New York was from Kansas City. The map's legend had a small note underneath the mile scale: *one inch equals approximately 250 miles*. There was a little over five inches separating the locations. "Arlo was right. It's about 1200 miles. If we can do about 600 today and tomorrow, we should be there before dinner tomorrow night. Zac traced Interstate 70, East out of Kansas City and into Pittsburg. "Looks like we stay on 70 East until we get into Steeler Country. Then go North a bit before jumping on 80 into New York," he concluded.

Alicia let out a dramatic exhale.

"What's up, Leesh?" Melany asked, taking notice.

"Z said, New York. We're going to New York! I bet it's one big city! With celebrities walking up and down the street like normal people!"

She had a point. The closest thing to a celebrity they had in Oklahoma was a large water tower that read: Home of Garth Brooks.

Alicia's star-struck excitement was contagious. "Hey, do you think we'll be able to get on MTV? They're covering *Woodstock*, right?" Paul asked, looking to Jax for answers.

"Dude, Z and I were talking about that shit the other day. We are *so* getting interviewed! Or, at the very least, we're crashing someone's interview," Jax said, while doling out random high-fives.

The cashier at the General Army Navy Outlet silently ridiculed the group of teenagers as they unloaded two, overflowing, shopping carts onto the conveyor belt. Zac flashed her with a lazy smile. She rolled her eyes in return. He couldn't tell if she was annoyed that she had to ring everything up first thing in the morning, or jealous that she wasn't going with them on what appeared, based on their supplies, to be a fantastic adventure. Zac chalked it up to being annoyed since her goth-like appearance did little to indicate she was the outdoors-y type. Once the large items, such as sleeping bags and tents, were scanned, she looked into the second cart as Paul began to unload glowsticks by the handful.

The cashier had the voice of an old lady with the body of someone in her early 20s, "You don't need to set all those sticks on the belt individually. I only need to scan one. How many did you get?" she asked Paul.

He hadn't counted. He'd grabbed from the shelf. He glanced into the cart. "Like, thirty, but they're all different colors—does that matter?"

There were more than 30; however, the cashier could have cared less, "What do you need that many glowsticks for?" she inquired.

"Tag!" Paul said excitedly.

The cashier blew a large, slow bubble with her gum.

Leaving the store, Melany mentioned she needed to call her parents to inform them she was safe.

Zac had forgotten to do the same. "That's a great idea," Zac said. The pair headed for the two payphones on the other side of the twenty-five-cent tiny horse ride.

Melany took the phone on the right. "See you momentarily, my love," she said, slowly releasing his outstretched arm.

"Can't wait," he replied.

"Barf," Jax chimed in with a crude gesture as he passed by. Fluttering his eyelashes, he added, "I'll be counting the minutes until both of your return. I can hardly wait."

Zac laughed, then pulled out the prepaid calling card Janis always made him carry in his wallet. It was almost 10 a.m., so after listening to the dreaded prompts, he tried his mom at work first. A familiar voice came over the receiver, "Sunshine Flowers, this is Janis—"

"Hey, Mom," he interrupted her before she could finish her usual welcome.

"Zachary Taylor! Where are you!?" She apparently hadn't forgotten that he had forgotten to call.

He told her everything—all the way down to the bitchy cashier in the Army-Navy store only moments ago. Despite all the information Zac had slammed her with, she seemed fixated on the fact that Arlo was a little person—a piece of information her older brother had failed to disclose to her as well. Zac thought for sure she would detest the fact he would be going to New York rather than returning home. And, she did. At least the part about going to *Woodstock '94* without a "real" adult chaperone. However, what could she say—no, don't? Their call was briefly interrupted by an operator, "You have—1 minute—remaining on your card." Janis only heard a pause. "Ma—I only have a minute left. I'll get another card and call when I can," Zac said quickly, trying to avoid getting cut off.

"Okay, baby! Be safe—I love you!"

Zac sat on the small electric horse, waiting for Melany to finish speaking with her folks. Winnie was taking up two parking spots in the back of a large empty lot. He could see his friends beginning a hacky sack session as they waited. He stood as he heard Melany say her goodbyes.

"Whatcha doing?" she asked, wrapping her arms around him from behind, placing her chin on his shoulder.

"Watching them." The cool morning air was turning into a heated afternoon. "Do you think he's proud of me?" Zac asked.

Melany leaned to her left, hoping to make some sort of eye contact. "Of course, he's proud of you, Zac. Look at those guys out there. Look at their smiles. We are having the times of our lives right now. Twenty-five years from now, we'll be sitting around thinking about how the summer before our senior year we went to *Woodstock*. Your uncle has been preparing you for this your entire life. I hate to admit it, but Jax was right last night. Uncle J taught us all how powerful music can be. You tie that up with the love we all have for each other—I promise—he's more than proud."

Zac squeezed her hands, "You know, he called the morning of my 18th birthday. I was in a hurry, so I didn't talk to him much. But he collaborated with my mom to surprise me that night. When my mom told me he wasn't coming at breakfast, I was so mad. All I wanted was for him to show up—if only for a minute. Now, I wish he wouldn't have..." Zac did his best to hold back his tears.

Melany moved to stand in front of him. "Baby, you couldn't have known!" she said, doing her best to provide him comfort.

"I miss him, Mel—I really miss him."

She held him tighter. "I know, baby—but you're doing what he'd want you to do. This has your uncle written all over it."

He spun Melany around and dipped her, trying to lighten the mood, "Why, Melany, you're not wearing a bustle," he said.

She caught the twinkle in his eye. A look that made her feel safe, respected, and most importantly: loved. Smiling, she replied, "I love your Doc Holiday voice, you movie-quoting, mother-fucker."

Zac laughed.

CHAPTER 21

Clogged Pipes

The sun was setting as Double drove Winnie across the Pennsylvania state line with Alicia sitting shotgun. "You're telling me Loo-Kee is She-Ra's spirit animal?" Double asked, handing Alicia the half-smoked joint the two shared.

Alicia laughed, "Yes! That's what I'm telling you."

Jax sat at the table, trying to get stems from the weed he'd cut up from under the Grateful Dead decal, "What the fuck are you guys laughing about up there?" he asked.

"Do you remember Loo-Kee?" Double asked, glancing at the rearview mirror to make eye contact.

Jax looked at Paul, signaling, *who the hell is Loo-Kee?*

Paul shook off the question.

"You guys remember She-Ra—right?" Alicia probed.

The two replied yes with a head nod. "Loo-Kee was the blue-haired elf that you had to find hidden in the trees and bushes at the end of the episode."

Paul snapped his fingers like it was some magical way of summoning forgotten information, "Oh, yeah! I remember that. I never knew where that fucker was hiding."

Alicia walked by on her way to the restroom. "I was telling him that Loo-Kee is She-Ra's spirit animal."

Paul whispered to Jax after Alicia closed the door, "Dude, what's a spirit animal?"

Double scanned through radio stations trying to fill the dead air. "The Sign" by Ace of Base was in its final choirs. The DJ said *Woodstock '94*, as Zac and Mel emerged from the sex den.

"Turn that up!" Melany shouted, fixing her hair.

"Traffic is beginning to pile up heading into Saugerties for the 25th Anniversary of Woodstock. The iconic musical festival is expecting crowds in the upper 500-Ks this weekend, and with that comes a lot of delays. If you're planning on battling the traffic, make sure you plan accordingly. State Troopers informed us that exits 80 to 83 are your best bet as they do their best to keep things moving along. However, it comes as no surprise that most Americans are flocking to experience three more days of peace, love, and rock 'n' roll. Keep it right here on New York's only station that has sticks with wicks, *98.5 The Match*!"

Melany could hear Alicia stomping in the restroom with excitement. Hearing the announcement had reignited their enthusiasm. "You okay in there?" Melany asked, knocking on the door.

"I think I might have peed a little!" she replied with a laugh.

This was the first broadcast regarding *Woodstock* they had heard—a sure indication that they were one step closer to their destination. Almost as if on cue, Double yelled for everyone to look out the front windshield. A, newer, blue hatchback car flew past them in the left lane. In the rear window, someone had drawn a large flower with shoe polish. Above the flower read: *Woodstock Bound.*

Zac put his arm around Melany, "Think it's a sign?!"

The restroom door opened with a gagging sound. The odd noise captured everyone's attention. Alicia couldn't escape the room fast enough as a God-awful stench of human feces followed her into the galley.

"Did you shit?!" Paul asked.

Melany turned and slugged him in the shoulder. "Paul!" she yelled.

Paul held his arm in discomfort. "*What?* It smells like she shit!" he replied.

She pushed him, but the foul smell had set off a chain reaction of gagging. Alicia couldn't stop, "I can smell it in my hair!" she said.

Zac leaned over to sniff her—the smell was hovering in the vehicle. He couldn't smell it *on* her. "What is that?" Zac asked.

Alicia slid open the window above the table and pushed her face out of Winnie as far as the screen would allow. "I think you're out of water. The toilet won't flush, and I couldn't wash my hands," she said, struggling not to vomit.

Jax and Zac opened all the windows.

Paul lit a joint.

"Why are you smoking a joint right now, Paul?" Melany asked.

Paul exhaled, "It smells better than that shit!"

Melany gave him a *that makes sense*, look.

"Dude, when was the last time you filled this thing up with water or dumped the pooper?" Paul asked.

Zac stared at everyone mystified. "What do you mean?" he replied.

Paul let out a fake laugh. "Plumbing, Z. Not sure if you noticed or not, but this thing isn't hooked up to the city like that shitty apartment of yours."

Zac didn't have a clue on the do's and don'ts of a recreational vehicle.

"Man, how would I know all that!? I literally got it *three days ago.*"

He had a point. This was his first time ever being in one, much less taking care of one.

Paul had Zac follow him to the microwave. Mounted under the range was a long black piece of plastic with multiple buttons and unlit lights. Paul said, "This here is your control panel." It was the same lesson Paul's grandfather had given him a couple of summers ago on a camping trip in Napa Valley. He pointed out the words: grey, black, and fresh. Each word had a light next to it and, depending on if that particular tank was full or not, dictated which color the light would be. Green for near empty, or empty, and red for near full or full. Grey was used for shower and sink tanks. Black was for the toilet, and fresh was drinking water. Zac got the idea and did his best to hurry the lesson along, as the smell of human waste got stronger with each passing minute.

Double pulled off the first exit he could. They were in the middle of nowhere, and there wasn't another vehicle or store in sight. The main door flew open the moment Winnie came to a stop, with everyone exiting a fast as possible. "Was it full?" Double asked, walking around the front of Winnie to join his friends. "The pooper is full, and it's out of water," Paul said.

Jax scanned the terrain. There wasn't anything except woods for miles in every direction. "So, what do we do? We have a few water jugs we could pour in there."

Paul shook his head no. "You can't dump water jugs in there, that will fill it up more. We need to connect a water hose to it to replenish it."

Melany went back inside. They watched her walk into the sex den, and heard her unzip a bag.

"What are you doing, Mel?" Zac shouted.

She didn't reply. Her steps seemed to get faster with every passing second.

"Uhhh…" Zac said, standing on his tip-toes.

Alicia scanned Zac up and down, then tried to mimic him to see what Melany was up too.

Melany came barreling out of Winnie, gasping for fresh air.

"Were you holding your breath that entire time?" Double asked as Melany bent over, struggling for air.

She nodded.

"What did you do?" Alicia asked. "I lit a candle I brought with me and put it in there. Hopefully, that will help the smell until we can fix it." Double initiated the round of high-fives she received. "Well done, girl!" Doubled added.

The group sat alongside the road and smoked while waiting for the scent of mulberry to smother the shit stench Winnebago. Alicia exhaled and asked everyone, "Why did Tigger look in the toilet?" Blank stares focused on her question.

"No clue," Paul said. An answer everyone agreed with.

"He was searching for Pooh!"

The group erupted with laughter. Maybe it was the weed, or possibly their current predicament, but her joke was well received by all. Once the laughter died down, she told everyone that her little brother had told her family that joke at her great-grandmother's 95th birthday party. When her great-grandma heard her cute little five-year-old grandson tell everyone, she laughed so hard her dentures flew out of her mouth. Her brother thought his joke was the funniest thing ever. He had no idea that their great-grandmother lost her teeth over it.

Cautiously they all filed back inside. The candle had done nothing to decrease the smell. In fact, it had made it somewhat worse as it now smelled like someone had taken a giant mulberry shit. Sitting still for a while instead of churning the tanks while driving down the road had taken the edge off, but as soon as they hit the road again it would be as bad as ever.

Zac turned to Paul, "So…what's the play, master-camper?" he asked.

Paul welcomed the nickname. "We drive until we find somewhere to dump and pump," Paul replied.

Jax interrupted, "Wait. We're supposed to drive around, searching for somewhere to dump that shit? Why don't we do it right here?" It was dark, and they had no idea if they would even find somewhere with the facilities required to dispose of human waste properly. Jax continued to plead his case, "No one is around. We dump that shit out on the side of the road, get rid of that smell, and fill up with water at our next stop." He heard crickets. "All in favor say—I!" he added with his hand raised.

Everyone hesitantly raised their hands.

Jax grabbed a flashlight from the camping gear and followed Paul outside while everyone else watched from the sofa. "Do you know what you're doing?" Jax asked as Paul popped a black cap off of the rear bumper.

"I have a pretty good idea," he replied confidently as he pulled a coiled hose from inside. He told Jax that this is pretty much the same setup as his grandfather's rig. Maybe a few years newer. He handed Jax the hose in exchange for the flashlight.

"What do you want me to do with this?" Jax asked, puzzled to why he was holding the hose. "Your idea, your job!" Paul replied.

"The fuck you say! I don't know what to do. You're the master-camper—remember?"

Paul agreed, "Yeah, but you have two hands. My one makes for the perfect flashlight holder. Don't worry, little fella, I got your back."

They walked to the driver side of the Winnie, almost directly below the window that the rest of the crew was watching from. Paul instructed Jax on how to connect the hose, then showed him the lever to release to remove the waste. He told Jax that he'd be able to feel everything running out of the tube once things began to flow.

Jax did as he was told. Everything connected as expected. However, when he pulled the lever, nothing happened. Jax turned to Paul, "Now what?"

Paul shined the light, ensuring the connection was secure. Everything appears to be secured properly. "It should be flowing?" Paul said.

Jax snatched the flashlight from his grasp.

"What's going on down there?" Alicia asked concerned.

They couldn't see either of them, only increments of beaming light, shooting to the sky.

"Nothing, it's clogged," Paul replied.

Jax stretched the hose out to its limit, hoping that would get things moving. Nothing.

"Hey, go grab that broom in the closet next to the fridge," Jax said.

Alicia heard the request and had it waiting for Paul as he pulled open the door.

He handed it to Jax who coiled the hose back up and inserted the broomstick, hoping to dislodge whatever was obstructing their progress. He was only able to insert the broom halfway before he felt resistance. "You hear that?" he asked Paul, as the sound of the tip of the stick banging on something solid rang out.

"What do you think it is?" Paul asked.

"No idea." Jax stretched the hose to its limits once again.

"How's it looking, baby?" Alicia shouted as he came into view.

"Good, I think," he replied, without a clue on his progress. He shined the light into the hose, hoping to see the obstruction.

"You see anything?" Double asked.

Jax had difficulty seeing inside the hose while simultaneously shining the light down it.

"I got nothing!" Jax yelled.

Double stepped into the restroom.

"What is he doing?" Melany asked.

Double leaped into the air inside the restroom. The thud from his brutal landing rattled everything inside and outside Winnie.

Startled, Paul accidentally pulled the second, smaller lever on the tanks outside.

Jax heard the familiar sound of water gushing down a hose before exiting, much like when he filled the kiddy pool every other morning for the city. It happened too fast. A burst of warm, muddy piss slammed into his face!

Paul pinned himself against Winnie, doing all in his power to avoid the same fate of his shit-covered friend.

Screams of, "Drop the hose, Jax!" echoed from inside.

Desperate to escape, Jax jumped backward out of his sandals, slipping and sliding in an endless spout of God knows whose shit. "I've got AIDS in my mouth! I've got AIDS in my mouth!" he screamed, removing clumps of soggy toilet paper clinging to his chin.

Paul picked-up the broom, extending it out as far as he could in hopes of a rescue. It was no use. The more Jax struggled, the more he slipped. This was one shit storm he'd have to ride out.

Double hurried back into the living area, thinking he heard screams of achievement. "Did that help?" he asked.

Alicia, Melany, and Zac didn't even look at him as they stared out the window. "If help is what you want to call it." Zac said, unable to take his eyes off of the spectacle outside.

Double looked over Alicia's shoulder. "Oh—that's nasty!"

The waste coming out of the hose was finally down to a small trickle.

Instead of helping Jax to his feet, Paul held out the broom handle. Jax took hold and Paul slid him across the slimy grass to a dry spot. Paul began to speak, "Um..."

Jax held up his hand as shit rolled off his elbow. "Not a fucking word!" Jax demanded, standing to his bare feet.

The rest of the crew crept out of Winnie.

Alicia blinded Jax with her flashlight, "Baby!" she said, never contemplating hugging him for comfort.

Jax stood in the middle of the road. "I need the eight gallons of water we brought, a bar of soap, and shampoo—and I need it right now!" They all scrambled, doing their best to avoid eye contact for they knew they would lose their shit, like Winnie, with laughter.

CHAPTER 22

California Sunshine

It was the morning of August 11th. The crew had topped Winnie with water when Melany yelled out, "Driver!" as they exited the Wal-Mart service station. After purchasing some last minute supplies—specifically replacing the gallons of water Jax had used to bathe the previous night, they found themselves crossing the New York state line. A large green sign read from top to bottom:

Informing them of their arrival.

Only miles from their destination, Zac fumbled with a map as he played navigator.

Double and Paul broke out the dominoes Double had bought during their stop, while Jax and Alicia walked into the sex den to nap.

"No sex in my bed!" Zac yelled.

Jax flipped him off and shut the partition behind him.

Dominoes, or bones, as they referred to it, was a game everyone on board enjoyed playing. They picked up the game after watching Boyz in the Hood in the summer of 1991. Something about watching Ice Cube slam his last "bone" on the table and shout, "Domino motherfuckers!" had captivated them, and they had been hooked ever since. Paul wasn't as big of a fan as the rest of them, mainly because he wasn't able to hold the seven bones, one starts the game with, in his hands like his friends. He had to prop them up on the table in front of him to see his tiles. They often called his gramps because of it. He looked like an old man when he played. Jax always harassed him, saying he played like an old man. Old man or not, he was a great ally to have sitting across from you when they played teams.

Double flipped over a random tile to see who would play first. Whoever flipped the highest one, began the game and had the advantage to domino first. Double flipped the 2/3.

Paul smiled at him. "Sucker!" he said, believing he could beat the 5 points. Paul turned over the double blank, totaling 0 points.

"Who's the sucker now, bitch!" Double replied laughing.

Paul took his consolation prize: the loser had to shuffle the bones. After pulling his seven tiles from the shuffled pile, Paul asked, "Play to 500?"

Double chose his tiles as well. "Naturally," he replied, as he started the game by laying down the 5/5 spinner, knocking twice on the table, informing Paul he scored 10 points on the play.

Paul, who also had to keep score because of his loss, said, "So it's like that?"

Double gloated.

After two rounds, Double was winning by 55 points. "So, tell me about those California girls, bro!" Double insisted.

Paul scanned his tiles for one to play. "Man, there was only one girl, but she turned out to be a flake. She didn't find life as humorous as I do, so I threw her back in the sea, now I'm looking for a new fish."

Double probed for more, "Do tell."

Paul went on to tell him he was "with" the girl who had turned him on to Papa Roach. They had been seeing each other since the beginning of summer. During his last weekend in California he had heard there was a fancy movie theater in San Francisco, one that had a stadium-like seating; however, what made it elegant was the fact that the chairs were recliners and they had servers who brought concessions to the customers. They called it a "Big Screen Bistro." It was cool because people didn't have to wait in line, they got their tickets, then reclined in their chairs as waiters came to them. Paul thought he'd surprise his summer crush by spending the day touring San Francisco, then dinner while they watched *Forrest Gump*.

The day went as planned for him. The two were having the time of their lives—or so he thought. They spent most of the day at Fisherman's Wharf, watching the street performers do their thing, then seals sunbathing on the docks. Paul described it as "the perfect day." However, at the theater, things took a turn for the worst. Paul purchased their tickets at the front counter, as his date stood, waiting near the arcade. Walking over to his partner, he scanned his tickets, 13, seats E11 and E12, so the two headed to theater 13. They sat in their assigned seating a little before 4:30, with the show starting at 4:40. Previews played as their server brought them their food. The two sat and chatted quietly as they devoured a small pepperoni pizza.

Paul looked at his watch after what seemed like the hundredth preview played: 5:10. He turned to his date, "Have you ever been to a movie where there were this many previews?" he asked. As his date shook her head no, a man with his young daughter approach his seat, "Um—I think you guys are in our seats." Paul looked up at the man like he was an idiot. He pulled out his tickets to verify, "Nah, man, this is us." Showing him the E11 and E12. The man pulled out his tickets as well. His too had E11 and E12 printed on his. However, when Paul glanced at the man's ticket, it read: "*Lion King*, at 5:20 p.m." Paul instantly looked at his a second time, his date was pulling on his arm, curious as to what was going on. Paul turned to her, wearing an I fucked up look on his face and informed her they were in the wrong theater altogether.

When he originally scanned the ticket, he focused on the 13; however, his finger was covering up the "PG." So, he assumed they were in theater 13—an honest mistake, he thought. The two stood as the man and daughter took their seats. As they exited the theater, Paul informed his date their movie was actually in theater 4. Paul could tell she was upset. Knowing they missed over thirty minutes of their film, he pleaded his case, telling her that they would have a story for the rest of their lives. He always tried to turn a negative into a positive—a trait his friends admired him for. His date found no humor in it, though. When he dropped her off that night, she told him she didn't think their relationship would pan out, "and that is was that. I never saw her again," Paul said.

Double sat confused, looking across the table at his friend. "You sat through 30 minutes of previews? Don't you think after 10 minutes you should have inquired?"

Paul shrugged off his question.

Double added, "I think you've got your facts twisted, homie. Sounds like she threw *your* ass back in the sea!"

Paul stared at his tiles. "To-ma-to, To-ma-to!"

Melany had driven a ¼ mile in two hours when they came across their first Woodstock road sign that informed them they had 20 miles to go. Traffic was back-to-back, resembling the music video "Everybody Hurts" by R.E.M. Everyone sat in their vehicles, staring at their surroundings, daydreaming about God knows what. Some jumped out of their cars to snap photos of themselves underneath the make-shift Woodstock road sign.

Melany looked at Zac, who stared at his map of New York, "How's it look?" she asked, noticing he'd look at the map, then out the window, then back to the map.

Zac shouted to the crew, "What exit did the radio say to take yesterday?"

Jax and Alicia, who had gotten comfortable on the sofa, shrugged their shoulders.

"Fourscore!" Double yelled from the back.

Everyone turned to him. "What the hell is fourscore?" Paul asked, looking up from his titles.

Double returned the same confused look. "You guys don't know what fourscore means?" For his own sanity, Double had to know how deep "the rabbit hole" went. "You guys know who Abraham Lincoln is—right?" he asked. He knew they did; however, he was playing this conversation like he would a game of chess, thinking three or four moves ahead. His question was met with nothing but eye rolls. "Do you guys know the name of his most famous speech?" he asked, still having his fun.

Paul, bit, "It was some sort of address, right?"

Double laughed. "Damn, Paul—you're sharp as a tack today."

Paul felt the sarcasm.

Melany helped her stumbling friends, "It's called the Gettysburg Address, and he gave it on November 19, 1863; a few months after the Union defeated the Confederacy."

Zac looked at his girlfriend with amazement.

"*What!?* I wrote a paper on it in History, freshman year," she added.

Double was impressed too. "That's correct, Mel—well played." He then proceeding to inform them President Lincoln began the Gettysburg Address with "Fourscore and seven years ago." What he was actually saying was that our forefathers had dedicated the proposition that all men were created equal 87 years prior. "So, you see, fourscore means 80, you want to take Exit 80," he said, gloating.

The crew glared at him, mouths agape.

Alicia was the first to speak, "Well *that,* I did not know! How do you know all that Mike?"

Double smiled. "Abe's my favorite Pres. And don't feel bad. I bet most of America doesn't know what it means."

Jax' temper got the best of him, yet again. "Why the fuck wouldn't he say that? Why come up with some crazy shit like fourscore and seven years ago!? I hate shit like that."

Double laughed again. "It's called being educated, Jax."

Jax flipped him off. "My bad! Must be that Oklahoma public-school education I've received. Mel—please take exit fourscore. If you miss it, take exit fourscorty-one. Fucking stupid!"

When they made it to Exit 80, there were state troopers directing traffic.

Melany rolled down her window.

"You heading to Woodstock, or passing through?" The officer asked with a thick Northeastern accent.

"Woodstock," Melany replied with a smile. "Follow that blue RV in front of you."

Alicia stuck her head between the two captain's chairs up front. "Do you think everyone from New York sounds like that?" she asked.

Melany laughed. "I felt like we were going to get whacked by the mob or something," she said.

They weren't moving much at all; however, hearing the officer ask if they were there for Woodstock was surreal; they still couldn't believe they were in New York.

Melany followed the blue RV into a gravel parking lot. There were four men in bright yellow vests directing people where to park. The lot was relatively empty, considering the traffic they had spent the last four hours in.

"This must be one of many lots?" Zac said, unbuckling his seatbelt.

"Where's Woodstock?" Alicia asked, looking out the window behind the sofa.

"Good question," Zac replied.

Melany put Winnie in park.

Everyone stood and stretched. They felt like there should be a big celebration, but there was nothing. People were still arriving. No one was out walking around. There were no parties. There was absolutely no sign that the biggest concert of the century was about to take place tomorrow. Double and Jax grabbed three lawn chairs a piece from the closet next to the fridge.

"Let's kick it outside and see what happens," Double said.

Zac held Melany back. "You guys go ahead. We'll make some sandwiches and be out in a few," he said as everyone stepped out.

Melany looked confused as everyone filed past her to step outside.

Zac smiled, "Sorry, I don't know when I'll get time with you alone next, and I'm hungry.

Melany blushed, but it was welcomed.

The parking area smelt different than they had expected when stepping outside. The almost empty lot was surrounded by trees for as far as the eyes could see, yet the scent of a forest was absent. The smell of pine was in the air, but it was blanketed by what they could only conclude to be pollution, as if there were a city nearby. The blue RV they had followed had the same idea as Double. A tall, long brown haired man wearing a Doors t-shirt and blue jeans began to unload folding chairs from the back of his RV. They exchanged head-nods, but no words.

"Nice people," Paul said as the man, who appeared to be close to their age, disappeared to the front of his vehicle.

Cars filed in at a steady pace as Zac and Melany handed out sandwiches and joined everyone under the awning Paul and Jax had set up. The sun was setting on the west side of the lot.

"You guys want to walk around and scope out the land for tonight's game?" Double asked.

Paul jumped out of his chair. "Shit! I almost forgot!" he said, disappearing inside Winnie.

"What's up with him?" Melany asked.

Before anyone could reply he returned. "Alright, I need all of you to close your eyes and open your mouths. No questions asked—do it!" Paul commanded.

They complied.

Paul stepped in front of each of them one at a time, placing small squares on their tongues. "Okay—open them," he said. They all looked at each other, curious as to what Paul had given them. "Happy birthday, Z!" Paul shouted.

They were still looking to each other for answers.

"It's the California Sunshine I brought back from Cali," Paul said, elated for what was to come.

Melany panicked, "You gave me acid! Should I spit it out!?" she asked.

"Too late now," Jax said.

"He's right, Mel. If it's good, it won't take long to get into our systems.

Melany had never dropped acid before. "Paul if I die, I'm gonna kill you!"

They all looked at her, trying to process.

"You know what the fuck I mean!" she added.

About fifty yards behind Winnie, they discovered a dirt trail that led to a run-down sports field. There was a worn-down backstop that appeared to host little league baseball, or perhaps softball, once. To the left of the barrier, was one set of metal bleachers with four rows of seats. Lines of cars began to park on one side of it. However, the opposite side was unused. In the distance, there were four old wooden telephone poles outlining the end of the field. Each appeared to have been sitting a while. Almost like whoever placed them there had intentions of constructing something but, perhaps, lost funding. "This is perfect!" Paul said.

Alicia stared out into the same field, "What are you guys doing again?"

Paul pointed to the open field, and said, "If you play it, they will come!"

She still looked confused.

"We're going to play tag," Jax said, trying to help her out.

On the way back to Winnie they were able to recruit a handful of players. Mostly because others were curious as to what the hell a bunch of Oklahoma kids were talking about.

Paul explained the rules to everyone as they all bent the glowsticks, making them illuminate. The game was played much like dodgeball. All of the glowsticks would be placed in the middle of the field. Half of the players lined up about 25 yards from the center of the field, with the other half taking their places at the opposite end. When someone yells go, the brave souls charge for the glowsticks, hoping to recover as many as they can. Those that possess glowsticks hurl them as hard as they can at all the other players. If someone is hit, they are out until the next round. If an opposing player catches a glowstick that has been thrown at them, the person that threw the glowstick it out. The game is played until only one person is left standing. The most significant difference between dodgeball is the fact that the glowstick can hit 60 to 70 miles-per-hour, depending on the strength of the thrower. Which in turn can cause a lot of pain and suffering, especially if hit in the face. The game is best played on acid because of the tracers that come off the glowsticks as they fly through the night sky.

Zac noticed the guy from the blue RV listening to Paul explain the rules and approached him, "How did he con you guys into playing?"

"Well, my buddies and I dropped acid when we pulled in. Your friend here said he had a game that would take our trip to a whole new level."

Zac smiled, he knew exactly what Paul was referring to. "Oh yeah, you won't want to miss this. It's an acid-trippers heaven." The long-haired man looked at him inquisitively, "You tripping too?" he asked. "Yeah, we also dropped when we got here."

"Nice. I'm Roger. Everyone calls me Rog."

Zac returned the introduction. "Hey, just don't get caught up in the tracers. The second you do, you'll get drilled—hard!"

Rog shook his head. "I take it you've played a few times," Rog asked.

Zac held a glow stick to his cheek. "See the scar below my eye? A blue glowstick. Took four stitches."

A look of panic blanketed Rog's face. "Fuck, dude. I don't think I want to play anymore." he said. "Protect yourself at all times. You'll be fine," Zac added.

The moon had replaced the sun, and 25 players took their positions. On the sidelines stood another 100 or so observers. Curious as to why there was a pile of glowsticks in the center of a field with people standing around them. Zac stood next to Melany, both eagerly awaiting Paul's instructions to begin. Their trip was in full effect. The glowstick in the center of the field looked like a ball of energy to them. They were smiling uncontrollably. Zac looked over to Mel, "You ready for this, baby?" he asked, noticing a possessed look in her dilated eyes.

"You mother-fuckers are dead!" she yelled.

Zac laughed.

She glared at him with a *why the fuck you laughing* expression.

For the first time, Zac was terrified of her.

Paul shouted, "On your mark! Get set! Go!"

Everyone made a mad dash toward the pile of multi-colored glowsticks. It was every man, or woman, for themselves. Friends or not, everyone was an enemy. Zac was able to snatch three sticks from the pile, throwing them at his opponents as fast as he retrieved them, quickly eliminating three people from the competition. He bent over, attempting to grab another. As he stood up, a stabbing pain overwhelmed his spine.

"Fuck-Me!" he yelled. His thin black t-shit did little to absorb the blow. His shoulder blades felt as if they were touching as the blow tensed him up. He reached with his right hand, trying to rub out the sting. Turning around to see who had eliminated him, the woman of his dreams stood behind him.

"You're out, mother-fucker!" she yelled as she acted like she was slitting her throat.

Zac didn't know whether to laugh, run away in fear, or be wildly turned on. She was like the spawn of Satan.

Zac took a seat next to Rog on the bleachers. "They got you too I see." Zac said, still trying to hold his back.

Rog was mesmerized by the tracers that streaked across the moonlit sky. "Yeah, man–some crazy chick beamed me in the neck and ran off screaming.

Zac made an *eww* face, for he knew how bad those type of hits hurt. "You were right, man. This is the craziest shit I've ever seen," Rog said. "How did you come up with this?"

Zac told him they had invented it by accident. Telling him that they had dropped once at a party, and Paul had pulled a glowstick out of his truck. They began by tossing it to each other, watching the tracers soar through the sky. Then Double got upset at Jax for something, and he threw it as hard as he could at him. The next time they did it, they had about 10 sticks. This was the only other time they had played and was by far the biggest game to date.

A glow stick whizzed by in front of them. As it passed by Zac heard a familiar voice yell, "Holy Fuck!" to his left. Double laid on his back, holding his face. "Dude, are you alright?" Zac asked, hovering above him.

Double's legs were kicking like a little kid throwing a tantrum, "Am I hurt? Am I hurt?" he screamed.

Zac stood over him. "How the fuck would I know if you're hurt or not? It hit you, not me!" Zac replied.

Double removed his hand from his cheek, "Am I bleeding?"

Zac laughed. "Dude, you're black, and I can't see shit in the dark."

Rog held up the green glowstick that beamed Double in the face, "Holy shit!" Rog said.

"Oh fuck, Z, how bad is it?"

Zac laughed. "Man, you're fine. It's just a flesh wound."

Zac helped Double to his feet. "Double, Rog—Rog, Double," he said, introducing the two.

Rog shook his hand. "You got me, man. I thought half my face was falling off when you said holy shit."

Rog laughed. "Had to try, right!"

Zac leaned over to Double. "You see any of the crew?" he asked.

Double scanned the crowd as they waited for the next round. "Man, it's as dark as my ass out here. I don't see any of them."

Rog and Zac laughed.

Rog sat in the middle.

"So where you from, Rog?" Double asked.

It took a minute for Rog to respond, the shooting glowsticks still fascinated him. "Um…sorry! Rapid City, South Dakota," he replied. "How about you guys?"

"Weatherford, Oklahoma," Double replied.

Rog took his eyes off the game. "Where the fuck is that?" he asked.

They laughed. "It's almost directly in the middle of the state. About 60 miles West of Oklahoma City." Zac stated.

"Where is Rapid City?" Zac asked.

Rog thought for a second, trying to think of a city as big as their Oklahoma City reference. "You guys ever hear of Mount Rushmore?" he inquired.

"Of course," Double replied. "We're about 20 miles or so from there."

Double found the conversation ironic. "Random question, Rog. Do you know what fourscore means?"

Zac thought to himself, *no way does he get this right.*

Rog looked over at Double. "Like, from the Gettysburg Address, fourscore?" Rog asked.

Rog was already proving to be brighter than Zac, and Zac noticed Double laughing to himself inside. "Yeah!" Double said.

"It means 80. He was referring to 87 years ago when he gave that speech."

Double gave him a high-five. "You alright with me, Rog! You alright with me!" And with that, Double had befriended the young man from South Dakota.

The first round lasted over 20 minutes. By the time they had gotten to the third and final round, the number of players had tripled. Double was the only one that had visible wounds from battle, though. Everyone else escaped with reminders that could easily be covered with clothing. None of Zac's crew was the last standing in either round; however, they all took pride in the fact that some country kids from Oklahoma were able to bring a game they created to New York. A game that they knew would follow both those that watched and played at home, no matter where that might be.

CHAPTER 23

Better Than Disneyland

Walking back to Winnie, the outside air smelled like dead skunk.

"Damn, I bet that's some good shit!" Paul said, referring to the strong weed smell. The lot where they had parked was now filled; there wasn't an empty spot to be had. Everywhere they looked, they saw lit cherry's from either cigarettes, joints, or some sort of drug being smoked. The party they were searching for upon arrival was in full swing. People walked around, greeting each other like they had known one another for years. There were no strangers here; it was easy to see Woodstock '94 was already shaping up to be more than a festival: it was becoming a movement.

The crew took seats under the awing. It was 9:30 and they were all at the peak of their acid trips.

"My stomach hurts," Melany said.

Zac assured her it was normal, something about the drug always made his stomach hurt as well. That, and his jaw seemed to tighten up.

Almost as if he had been chewing the same piece of gum for hours.

"It's the rat poison in the acid that makes your stomach hurt," Paul said from behind Melany.

She turned toward Paul. "You gave me rat poison!" Melany yelled.

Paul threw up his arms in defense.

Double interjected, "Man, that's an urban myth. People have been saying that shit since the 60s. Why the fuck would someone put strychnine in drugs? Ever heard of repeat customers? How the hell are dealers going to have people return for more if they kill them. Fucking rat poison. Ain't no rat poison."

Melany trusted Double, knowing he was the smartest of them all. "I'm just saying. I've heard that it's in there hundreds of times," Paul said, defending himself.

Double couldn't resist, "You think you're right—like that time you took ol'girl to the movie? You got that right too—didn't you?"

Paul held up his nub. "Don't think I won't nub a dude, motherfucker."

Zac interrupted their argument, "Are you at least having fun?" he asked.

Melany smiled. "That game was awesome! I think I liked watching more, though. The glowsticks flying through the air reminded me of when we used to stargaze as kids. Except these shooting stars were almost within our reach," she said, cuddling up to him.

Jax stepped inside. "Longview" by Green Day began to play as he came back out.

"Nice choice, brother!" Paul exclaimed.

Jax bowed. "Thank you. No applause, please," he said, lighting one of the joints he had rolled earlier.

Rog and his two buddies emerged from the front of their RV, each one holding a chair.

"Everyone, this is Dave and Eric. Dave and Eric, these are the games creators," Rog said.

Dave was the tallest of the three with Rog coming in a close second. It was difficult to see what they looked like, however, they both resembled Rog. They had long hair, and wore jeans and a t-shirt. Stepping into the light, Zac noticed Eric had a birthmark under his right eye—that, or he got hit really hard with a glowstick. Either way, he'd found a way to distinguish them.

Eric was the first to address the crew, "Man, that game was optical bliss! And Rog told us you guys invented it by accident—is that right?"

Double jumped out of his chair. "Oh—don't let these crackers take credit for it. I invented the game—out of my hatred for this mother-fucker!" he said, grabbing Jax by the neck.

Jax waived it off and told Double to sit his excited-ass down.

Double took a seat and asked, "So what's the plan for tomorrow?"

Zac leaned forward in his chair. "Rog, you guys hear anything about what to expect tomorrow?" he asked.

Rog told everyone that he heard they would be running shuttles to the stage starting at 8:00 a.m. He wasn't sure where the hub was for them, but assumed the crowds would lead the way.

It was the first Zac's crew had heard about the shuttles. It made sense, though. In their parking lot alone, there had to be almost 200 vehicles, and they had no idea how many lots there actually were. They only knew that the DJ yesterday on the radio said they were expecting somewhere in the neighborhood of 500K people, and figured there was no way people would be able to park near the stage.

"What time you guys heading over?" Paul asked.

"Rog looked down at the dirt for a second. "Man, we don't have tickets yet. Coming here was an impulsive decision. We figured there would be someone scalping tickets cheap, and we'd get in that way. That, or jump the fence."

Everyone laughed.

Everyone except Zac. He instantly heard Arlo's voice in his head regarding their chat about the universe always providing for "true" believers. It was a lesson his Uncle J preached constantly.

Zac stood up. "I'll be right back," he said.

Melany looked up at him. "You okay?" she asked, as he opened the screen door.

"Yeah, just need to grab something real quick." He shut the door behind him and walked into the sex den. In the side pocket of his backpack he retrieved the 10 tickets Arlo had given him. Nine of them were still attached to one-another. He sat on the edge of the bed. After counting four tickets, he folded the perforated side before the fifth ticket, tearing four of them from the pile. After that, he tore one off from the stack of four. He stood up, holding a solo ticket as he looked at himself in the only mirror in the room. Placing the sole ticket snuggly along the inside of the mirrors frame he whispered, *this one's for you, Uncle J.*

Zac exited Winnie and sat back down. Rog was sitting across from him, "Here you go, brother," Zac said, handing Rog three Woodstock '94 tickets.

Rog did a double take. "Dude, you have extra!?" he asked excitedly.

Zac nodded yes.

Rog held up the tickets to show Dave and Eric.

"Zac, let me pay you!" Rog demanded.

"No need, my friend. Just paying it forward."

Rog was confused. However, Zac didn't elaborate. He smiled, as he now knew why Arlo stipulated he had to give the extras away. He could see how much joy those tickets brought his parking-lot neighbors. Zac simply thought, *I could get used to this.*

Paul's rendition of Jax's clogged pipe incident had concluded the night with screams of laughter.

"Rog, did you tell them about the searches?" Eric said after he caught his breath from laughing so hard.

"Oh, yeah! We heard there are talks that they will be searching everyone tomorrow before allowing people on the shuttles. Not sure if you guys are planning on bringing any drugs or paraphernalia into the concert, but if you do, make sure it's not in something that will set off the metal detectors."

The thought of searches had never occurred to them. "Bro, thanks for looking out! We definitely will be taking some smoke in. Glad you said something," Double said, exchanging handshakes with Eric.

It was approaching midnight. "Alright all. I think we are going to try and get some shuteye. You guys want to hit the shuttles together tomorrow?" Rog asked. "For sure!" Zac replied, standing to send off his new friends.

"Zac, we can't thank you guys enough for the tickets, man. For real. I'm beside myself right now," Rog said, leaning in for a hug.

"Don't even mention it, man. Glad they're not going to waste," he replied.

Everyone said their goodbyes to Rog and his friends as they disappeared into the night.

"Well, ya'll—we ready to crash?" Zac asked.

Paul stood up as well. "Not sure I'll be able to sleep. I'm still tripping balls. But I'll try." Everyone agreed. Sleeping while still tripping posed a challenge. Yet, the next three days were going to be packed with things to do, and they knew they needed to rest.

Zac stared at the ceiling as the alarm clock buzzed at 6:00 a.m. He hadn't slept much. He was unable to turn his mind off. After shutting off the alarm clock, he woke Melany. She, on the other hand, had no problem falling asleep. "Baby, we should jump in the shower if we want hot water," he said, thinking about how they took a cold shower the day before. Twenty minutes passed before the two stepped into the tight shower together. "How did I not know you had this birthmark on your back?" Zac said as he stood behind her, kissing her neck. She moved to her left, trying to escape the tickles of his unshaven stubble.

"I'm sure there is a lot you're yet to learn about me," she said, looking over her shoulder. The smell of bacon entered the bathroom. "Double must be up." Zac said, making

Melany laugh. "Are you excited for Woodstock?" he asked, still trying to kiss her from behind.

"I'm excited to be at Woodstock with you," she replied.

He was thankful for that as well. For he couldn't imagine experiencing it without her. Exiting the bathroom, Zac saw everyone was up, and those that didn't shower last night were waiting their turn.

"I'd give it a couple of minutes, the water was getting cold while we were in there," Melany said, walking toward the sex den.

"How do you guys like your eggs?" Double asked as Zac followed Melany. "Scrambled!" they yelled.

"Scrambled eggs—coming up!" Double yelled

After eating the breakfast Double had prepared for everyone, Zac and Paul cleaned up, while Double and Jax got all the gear ready. Each of them had a backpack filled with all the necessities they would need for the next three days.

Zac pulled an envelope from his shorts pocket. "Here," he said, handing everyone $300 a piece. "If you need more, let me know. I'll put some extra in my secret stash."

Paul and Alicia didn't know about the stacks of cash Uncle J had left Zac. "Damn, Z! Did you rob a bank or something!?" Paul asked in a joking tone.

Zac laughed. "Nah, man! It's part of my inheritance." Zac could see Paul felt bad for his comment, "Dude, don't sweat it. It's all good! Let's have the time of our lives out there—and, for real—if you guys need more cash, say the word."

Jax sat at the table alone separating joints into three separate sandwich bags. "What's all this?" Zac asked, seeing what looked like hundreds of joints spread out across the table.

"I couldn't sleep last night, so I rolled two ounces," Jax said.

Everyone cracked up laughing.

Jax counted 151 joints total. "Here, odd man out, light that fucker up!" he said, handing joint number 151 to Double. Jax put 50 joints in each bag and handed one to Zac and Double. He lifted his jeans on his left leg and put the rolled up baggy in his sock. "You guys do the same. That way it won't set off the metal detectors if they have one," Jax said.

"Do you think this will be enough?" Double asked.

Jax looked up at him oddly. "Brother, I know you have a massive lung span and all, but have you ever, in your entire life, come close to smoking 50 joints in three days?"

Paul tried to hold his laughter back.

"Fuck you, Jax!" Double said.

There was a knock at the door.

"Must be Rog." Alicia said, peaking out the door window. She was right. Their friends from South Dakota had their backpacks on and were ready for Woodstock.

"Let's do this, bitches!" Jax said, with everyone jumping with excitement.

Alicia opened the door. "Morning guys!" she said, as everyone filed out of Winnie.

Zac was the last to step out, locking Winnie behind him.

"Hey, Double, will you make sure the front doors are locked, please?" he asked. "What up, ya'll?" Zac said, pulling the keys out of the deadbolt lock.

"Can you guys believe we're fucking going to Woodstock today?" Rog asked.

Jax was the first to reply, "Yes, I can!"

The answer stumped Rog and his friend, and an awkward moment of silence ensued.

"She's good!" Double said from the front of Winnie.

"Let's get this party started then!" Zac said. "We'll follow you, Rog." Zac added.

The weather could not have been better. The sun was out, and there wasn't a cloud in the sky. A lot had changed since they had first arrived. There were people coming from almost every direction. There were rows of cars where there shouldn't be rows of cars. Winnie, like Rog's RV, was packed in, there was no way they could exit the lot if they wanted to. Where there wasn't a car, there was an erected tent, or a tent being torn down—only to be erected on site. Herds of people marched East in clouds of smoke.

"I know that smell," Eric said with a smile.

They departed their parking area and followed the masses. "Man, I'm glad you guys told us about the busses and search parties. We would have been screwed," Paul said, handing Rog the joint Double had lit before they arrived.

"Shit, man! We're glad we met you guys. We'd still be looking for tickets," Rog replied.

Zac patted Rog's back. "You're family now, my man!" he said, taking the joint from him.

"Hey Paul, I know we're not supposed to ask, but what happened to your hand?" Eric asked.

It was a question Paul was accustomed to being asked. "When I was 5, my brother and I were chopping wood. I held my hand on the stump we perched the wood on, and I dared my older brother to take a swing. He called my bluff and swung. That fucker took my hand. You believe that!" Paul said, holding his nub just inches from Eric's face.

His answer literally stopped Eric in his tracks. He couldn't believe what he'd heard.

Zac stepped passed Eric. "He's fucking with you!" Zac said laughing.

Eric's face was expressionless.

"I don't know if it's okay to laugh or not!" Eric said, making everyone else laugh.

When Zac pictured the busses in his head, he visualized rows of Greyhound style busses. However, in the distance, he saw rows of yellow school busses lined closely together. As soon as one departed, another arrived. A cycle that appeared never ending.

"Look at all those people," Melany said. "There must be thousands of them," Alicia added.

Jax held everyone up. "Lets hold up a second and see how things are flowing," he said.

Rog patted his shoulder. "Good thinking!" he said, taking a seat to Jax's left.

"What all did you guys bring?" Dave asked.

"A bunch of joints. You?" Jax replied.

"Same, and shrooms," Dave added.

"Nice!" Double said.

Rog noticed security guards waving wands around concert-goers bodies. "You guys don't have any of your smoke in metal, do you?" Rog said, pointing to people being screened.

"Nah, man. Jax rolled it all up last night. We have it in our socks," Zac replied, watching his new friends eyes look down as if they'd be able to see through their jeans.

From what they could tell, guards were waving their wands and allowing people to pass. They couldn't see if people were actually being detained, or if they were having their stuff confiscated.

"Any of you guys see drug dogs?" Double asked.

A panic rushed through everyone.

"You don't think they have those down there do you?" Melany asked.

"I don't see any. Do you guys?" Zac said.

Everyone shook their heads no.

"Well, shit! Let's go to Woodstock then!" Melany said, bolstering with excitement.

Everyone laughed at her quick change in demeanor and followed her lead.

After standing in line for 20 or so minutes, Zac was the first to get searched. "How's it going?" he said nervously to the man waving a wand over his body.

"You have any weapons or illegal drugs on your person?" the man asked with the same thick accent of the trooper yesterday directing traffic.

Zac felt like he paused. "Um-no, sir!" he said, thinking, *please don't make me lift my jeans, please don't make me lift my jeans.*

"You're good. Next!" the man said, waving Melany to approach.

There was zero resistance. No one asked to see their tickets or anything.

Double leaned into Zac's ear and whispered, "Please tell me that's normal."

Zac laughed, and patted him on the back.

After everyone had been cleared to get on a bus, they did exactly that.

They were the second group to make it safely onto the bus they would ride to the site, and had their choice of seats. Melany was the first to step inside and took the seat all the way to the rear. They were barely able to squeeze two people to a seat because of the space their bags occupied. Alicia sat across from Melany.

"Look at all these trees! This definitely isn't a big city. Isn't it crazy when you think about how something will be in your head, only to find out that it's nothing like that once you get there?" she asked.

Melany agreed. "Nothing is ever like I picture it in my head," she replied.

"I thought we'd be in some open field in the middle of nowhere," Jax added.

"I'm sure the actual site will be open. Can't imagine they'd hold Woodstock where the stage could be obstructed by a tree line," Rog said.

Double turned around in his seat. "You guys know how long of a ride it is?" he asked.

Rog and his friends shook their heads no.

An older lady sitting in front of Double turned in her seat. "We overheard people last night saying it was about a 10-minute ride," she said.

"Sweet! Thank you!" Double replied.

The lady said, "Anytime," and turned back around to chat with her friends.

The bus was filled to max occupancy. Those who were able to get seats sat on their belongings, some of which stacked to the ceiling. The center isle was also packed with people standing with their bags as well. Zac thought to himself, *if there is an emergency, first responders are going to have a mess to deal with because of how much stuff people brought with them.*

No one spoke the entire 10-minute trip. Zac watched his friends as they stared out their windows, more than likely imagining the experiences to come, for that's what he did. Along the way, they saw crowds of people walking in the same direction the buses drove. Most likely those trying to elude the authorities—or hoping to sneak in, avoiding the $135 ticket prices. Nevertheless, Zac couldn't help but think how in only a few minutes, he and his friends would embark of one of the most memorable experiences of their lives. The bus began to slow down.

Melany squeezed Zac's arm tightly. "I'm so excited!" she whispered.

Zac grabbed her hand. "Me too! I can't believe this is real!" he replied.

Everyone began to stand and gather their things as the bus came to a complete stop in another parking area. The driver opened the door. "Welcome to Woodstock folks!" the driver said.

Everyone cheered.

Rashes of Goosebumps spread across Zac's body as he stood.

Zac bent down to see out the window. Looking outside he noticed hundreds, if not thousands, of people making their way up a steep grassy hill. It looked like there was some sort of sign on top of the hill. However, he couldn't be sure from his current location.

Rog and Double were the first of their group to exit the bus. In a hurry, they almost tripped each other as they desperately wanted to gaze upon the stage of Woodstock. Zac was the last to step outside.

Hey, Z!" Jax yelled, "If I didn't say it or if I forget to, I wanted to thank you for bringing me along. I'll never be able to repay you!" he said, with what looked like a tear in his eye.

Zac gloated. "This is all Uncle J, man!" Zac replied, looking up to the sky.

They all took a second to appreciate the gift Uncle J had given them. It was a gift they would cherish for the rest of their lives, and they didn't even know it yet.

Alicia looked up to the top of the hill. "What do you guys think is on the other side?" she asked.

"Woodstock!" Paul quickly replied.

"Well there's no sense in standing here with our thumbs up our asses. Let's do this, bitches!" Jax said.

Zac Taylor and his entourage moved along, like sheep following their Shepard, with the massive crowd of concert-goers, up the steep hill they believed was leading them to Woodstock '94. As they did so, they noticed everyone was pointing upward. Following the pointing fingers, almost simultaneously, they observed a tall white sign. The sign was still blurry from their current location, though.

"What do you think it says?" Jax asked.

They could hear other patrons asking the same question, each curious, not only with what the sign read but what might lay waiting for them on the other side of it as well. They continued to climb upward, feeling somewhat fatigued and gasping for air from the short hike. Suddenly, the words came into focus. It was a large white sign with dark blue lettering, standing about twelve feet high and ten feet wide, reading from top to bottom:

WELCOME TO WOODSTOCK '94
SAUGERTIES, NY

Chills rushed through Zac's body. He looked down at his right arm; every hair was standing erect, a feeling he commonly referred to as his "Spidey-sense." He gazed down and to his right at Melany's arm, who was firmly gripping Zac's hand, noticing the hair on her left arm was doing the same. Everyone that had made the journey, even those that Zac and his friends had recently met, all possessed similar facial expressions. They were smiling, yet these weren't regular everyday smiles, these weren't smiles of amazement and curiosity, they were smiles of arrival. They all stood directly underneath the welcome sign, in one line, side-by-side when Jax blurted, "This is better than Disneyland!" For a guy that had a habit of taking his comments to the extreme, Jax had nailed it.

Standing underneath the Woodstock '94 welcome sign, they looked in amazement at the massive North stage. It had two large screens on each side. Moving inward there were white doves perched on the neck of a guitar, exactly like the ones on their tickets. Centered above the stage was a blue and green globe. On one side it read "Wood" and on the other side "Stock." Jax couldn't contain himself, "Holy shit! That's John Popper from Blues Traveler," he shouted, pointing to the stage as they watched him jam to "But Anyway" on his harmonica.

People were flooding in and spanned as far as their eyes could see.

"What do you guys want to do first?" Melany asked, looking up at Zac.

He heard his uncle's voice:

Know where you're going, son, and know what you're going to do when you get there. You do that, and there is nothing you can't accomplish.

Zac knew he was going to Woodstock; however, as he grinned, he thought to himself, *what I'm doing while I'm here, well, that's an entirely different story…*

ACKNOWLEDGMENTS

John Roberts, Joel Rosenman, Artie Kornfeld, and Michael Lang—I haven't had the honor of meeting; however, without you guys, I would never have attended Woodstock '94, and Woodstock Bound would not exist. Thank you for having such a significant impact on the world and my life. If you end up reading this, I hope it puts a smile on your face.

My Brothers and Sisters In-Arms—I miss serving with you! Thank you, and your families, for your selfless dedication to protecting a country I love! I hope this novel provides you with some laughs to help pass the time, especially if you're deployed.

Air Force Wounded Warrior Program—You guys are amazing! Thank you for helping me transition into civilian life. I couldn't have done it without you!

Vanessa Anderson, aka "the editor"—You gave this novel a pulse! Thank you from the bottom of my heart! I cannot wait to work on the remainder of the Woodstock Bound series with you; it's going to be magical.

Carl Harrell—None of this would have happened had you not invited me to Woodstock '94. Thank you, brother! Can't wait for our next adventure.

Chad Horton—My oldest friend! Thank you for all your advice over the years. Your mentorship on this project was priceless, and I can't even begin to thank you enough.

Zachary Davis—Brother, you have been with me from the start. Thank you for teaching me the importance of character development. This story wouldn't have been as funny (as I think it is) without you.

Mom, Dad, Bill, Brittani, and Duane—I know I don't always show it, especially as of late, but I love you guys, a lot!

My Daughters—You two are the best thing that has ever happened to me! Thank you for allowing me to chase my dreams! Remember, dreams without action are just that, dreams! Make yours a reality! All you have to do is put in the work and be persistent; they will come to fruition.

My Wife—You are the only reason I'm here today. Thank you for everything you do for our family. I love you, baby!

FORTHCOMING

Zac Taylor and his crew will return in

Woodstock Bound: The Festival

Be sure to like/follow

on Social Media for Updates!

twitter.com/woodstockbound

facebook.com/woodstockbound94

ABOUT THE AUTHOR

STEVEN BATEMAN was born in Fairfield, California but lived his teenage years in Oklahoma after his father received military orders. He has degrees in Business Administration, Logistics Management, and Leadership Technologies. Shortly after attending Woodstock '94, he joined the United States Air Force, ultimately retiring from active duty in 2017. While he was committed to serving his country, he always dreamt of becoming an author; a dream he made a reality with his debut novel, *Woodstock Bound.*

www.ingramcontent.com/pod-product-compliance
Lightning Source LLC
Chambersburg PA
CBHW030618310726
48979CB00003B/775

* 9 7 8 1 9 4 9 1 9 3 7 8 7 *